Secret Love

Love Stings Series, Book 2

By Evan Grace

Secret Love

Limitless Publishing, LLC
Kailua, HI 96734
www.limitlesspublishing.com

Formatting: Limitless Publishing

ISBN-13: 978-1-68058-726-5
ISBN-10: 1-68058-726-9

Dedication

To all of my fans,
thank you for your never-ending support.

Chapter One

Carrington

The envelope in my hand is what I've been waiting for, and my nerves are shot as I stare at it. Inside are the results of my nursing boards, which will reveal if I can become a registered nurse. Even though I studied so hard for the test, it was brutal. When I finished, I went out to my car and bawled like a baby. I'm just glad my parents aren't home in case it's bad news. If I pass, then I can get a job at Lutheran Hospital as a nurse instead of working there as an aide. I love what I do, but being an ER nurse is my dream job and the pay is significantly better.

I slip my finger under the edge of the envelope and slowly drag my fingertip under and across it until it's completely open. I carefully pull the folded paper out, sit down on my bed, and unfold it. As I look it over, my heart sinks. I read the bold print words **HAS NOT PASSED** over and over. Tears immediately fill my eyes because again I'm a failure. I didn't pass.

I grab my laptop, quickly pull up the website to see when I can retake it, and swallow the lump in my throat when it says forty-five days. That's another two hundred dollars I'll have to pay. Dammit, this couldn't have happened at a worse time. Abby, my best friend and cousin, and I are moving in together. We've already put the deposit down on the new place, but there's no way I'll be able to afford it on my CNA wages. I have no clue what I'm going to do.

Before my parents or brother get home, I grab my bag and make my way out of the house. Seeing the look of disappointment on my parents' faces is the last thing I need right now. They already think I'm a fuck up, and this will just be the icing on the cake. I need to come up with a plan until I can take the test again.

***

I drive toward the hospital I work at in Charleston, contemplating my next move. I pull into the parking lot of The Thirsty Beaver Gentleman's Club. I've passed it so many times, but I've never really noticed it before. The place looks nice on the outside: paved parking lot, landscaped areas with various flowers, and shrubbery. There is even a little shelter area, maybe for smokers. The parking lot is well lit, and most of the cars are expensive looking.

I've met a few dancers before, and they always talked about how much money they made. I sit in my car and stare at the building in front of me. Could I do it? Could I take my clothes off in front of strangers? I've never been the shy type. I've been dancing in front of people since I can remember. I've always been an overly sexual person, so how hard could it be? My parents would freak the fuck out, but if I do this I won't tell anyone.

I'm not really dressed for a gentleman's club, I think as I look down at myself. Since I work at the hospital and change into scrubs there, I'm in my usual pre-work attire. Nothing fancy, just an off-the-shoulder t-shirt, cut-off jean shorts, and Chuck Taylor shoes on my feet—not your typical sexy outfit, but it'll work to just talk to the manager.

I take a deep breath and head inside. The slap of my shoes against the tiled floors echoes around me while I make my way down the short hallway that leads to a set of double doors that are so heavily tinted, I can't see inside. With a deep breath, I grab the handle and pull the doors open.

I've never been to a strip club before, so I wasn't sure what to expect. The strip clubs and gentleman's clubs in the movies always looked seedy, more like whorehouses. This one doesn't look seedy at all. A beautiful wood bar runs along one side of the building. Black and white leather furniture is spread throughout the space with matching tables. Booths line the perimeter.

There's one main stage with three different poles placed in various spots on the stage. Two smaller stages are on opposite sides of the main one. The DJ booth is in the corner, and I can see a guy standing up there. Right now, the music is a lot lower than one might expect. A group of men in suits are all sitting around one table with drinks in their hands. There's no one dancing, but a girl in a bikini is standing by the table of men.

"Can I help you?"

The voice behind me causes me to jump and then turn around. The woman is gorgeous. She has to be at least six feet tall. Her blonde hair is slicked back, giving the illusion of a Mohawk.

"Um, yes. Hi, I was wondering if you were hiring."

She looks me over and surprisingly makes me feel like a piece of meat. For a second, I think I'm imagining it until the woman very slowly lets her gaze travel down my body and then settle on my breasts. She bites into her lower lip before she looks back up at my face.

"Follow me." She starts walking toward the bar, so I follow behind her. My palms become sweaty as we step behind the bar and head down a hallway that leads to a huge office. "Have a seat. What's your name, sweetheart?" Her voice is husky, and she has a slight accent that I can't place.

"It's Carrington Carter."

"You want to be a dancer here?" I nod my head. "Have you danced before?"

"I've been dancing since before I could even walk. Now, I've never stripped before, but I don't have a problem showing off my body." I sound confident even though, under this woman's scrutiny, I'm feeling self-conscious.

"You are beautiful. Our customers are going to love you. I'm Bridgette, by the way, and I'm in charge of all of the girls. We don't need any more dancers right now, but we can always bring you on as a cocktail server until a spot opens up. You'll make sure the customers have full glasses, help serve during private parties, flirt, and make sure everyone is having a good time. What do you think?"

I'm a little disappointed that there are no dancer positions open, which I find odd. Don't most strip clubs take as many dancers as they can get?

"Okay, I'll take it."

She goes over my starting wage, which is pretty amazing. Plus, I'll get to keep all of my tips. She hands me an application and tells me to fill it out while she goes to get me my uniform. I fill it out quickly and am just finishing it up when she steps back into the office.

"All right, here you go." I take the pile of miniscule clothing from her. "We'll get you your own locker so you can change when you get here. When can you start?"

"I can start in two weeks. I just need to give my current job notice."

"Okay, let's have you come in two weeks from Thursday. You'll work Thursday, Friday, and Saturday nights. You get paid weekly, and of course you get to keep your tips. Any questions?"

"Um, no, I don't think so. I appreciate you giving me the job. I promise I'll do great."

She smiles, and again the way she looks at me makes me feel uncomfortable. Maybe she's a lesbian, and that's cool if she is, but I'm not into girls. Oh sure, I've kissed one once or twice, but it's just not my thing.

Before I leave, she takes me into the dressing room, where a couple of girls are sitting in front of mirrors that line the wall. They turn and look at me and then quickly dismiss me.

Bridgette shows me my locker and hands me the padlock with the combination. I hang my uniform, if the two little scraps of material could be called that, inside and shut and lock it. With a wave, I head out into the parking lot and climb into my car. Now I just need to go to work and tell them that I am dropping down to prn status, which means as needed and if I'm available, and I'll still keep my seniority.

As I make my way toward Charleston, I hope that the extra money I'll make will be enough. If not, hopefully a spot will open up for a dancer sooner rather than later.

***

I shove everything I'll need for the club into my bag: some makeup, makeup remover, toothbrush, and deodorant. On top of that, I throw in two pair of heels and my hair products. In preparation for my new job, I spent this past week getting my hair done and a mani and pedi. I even got spray tanned and waxed. Hopefully, the tips will be good. Otherwise I may not have enough to cover my portion of the bills for the apartment.

Bridgette called me yesterday to confirm I was still coming. Then she told me that I should get there early enough to get ready and be on the floor by eight. Thirsty Beaver can't possibly be busy that early, but maybe Bridgette wants me to come so early so they can show me the ropes. There's a knock at the door while I zip up my bag. I hear the door open and close.

Abby pokes her head in through the open door. "Hey you. Getting ready to head to work?"

Over a year and a half ago, we lived together in a different apartment, and one night while I was out, a monster followed her home and sexually assaulted her right in our living room. I had been on a date and had found her curled up on the floor when I got home. The images of her huddled up on the floor still plague me, and I can't even imagine what it's been like for her.

She was in such a bad state after it happened. She started using drugs, picking up skeezy guys, and having one-night stands until finally she tried to take her life. I thank the Lord that my uncle was home when she made the attempt and was able to get help before she succeeded. Abby's still not the same as she was before it happened, but I can slowly see her becoming the girl she used to be, or at least a modified version of that girl.

"Yeah. How was the studio tonight?" Abby teaches at the dance studio owned by our grandma. Now my mom and aunt Stacy run it.

"It was good. Those little girls are the most eager little things I've ever seen. There's this one, Natalie, who has to be my favorite. She's got the biggest attitude when she dances. It's adorable." A small smile touches Abby's lips.

"Are you sure you're going to be okay? I hate

7

leaving you here at night." Abby hates the dark, and usually, once the sun starts to set, she doesn't leave the apartment.

"I promise I'm okay. Your dad installed the extra deadbolt and the motion light outside the door. My dad's a phone call away. Don't worry about me; I promise I'm okay when you leave. You know me, I don't sleep that great anyway." Abby has terrible insomnia, and unless she takes a sleeping pill she's up and down all night. She wraps her arms around me. "Stop worrying, okay? I'm getting used to being here alone."

"Okay. Well, lock up behind me. I love you."

I hug her tight. She's two years older than I am, and we've been more like sisters than cousins. People assume I'm older than she is because I'm a good four inches or so taller than her. Abby's barely over five feet tall.

My palms sweat the whole drive to The Thirsty Beaver. The uncertainty about how the night is going to go is what's causing my stomach to twist and turn. I know how to flirt and I know how to tease, it's just something that comes easily to me, but is this going to be the kind of place where the men paw and grab at me all night? I guess I'll just have to see.

Once I reach The Thirsty Beaver, I park toward the back of the parking lot and under one of the lights. With a deep breath, I climb out of my car, grab my bag, and make my way inside. I can feel the vibration of the bass as I get closer to the double doors. Pulling them open, I step inside and look around. There's a woman in a thong twirling around a pole on the main stage. The place isn't filled up yet, but it's early. Most clubs don't start hopping until around ten, so I'm sure in time this place will fill up.

I find Bridgette by the bar talking to a man whose back is to me. She spots me and waves me over.

"Hi, Bridgette."

"Hi, doll." She turns to the man standing next to her. "This is the girl I was telling you about. Carrington, this is Rafe. He and his brother Tucker own this place. This is your new cocktail waitress, Carrington. Hopefully we'll be able to make her a dancer soon. Isn't she hot?"

I just stand there, mute. I have no clue what to say to either of them. He stares at me for a second before he lets his eyes travel up and down my body, and then he leans in.

"Welcome. I hope you like working here," he says near my ear. His hot breath causes goose bumps to pop up all over my skin.

"Rafe, leave her alone. She needs to get ready. Come on, Carrington."

She loops her arm through mine and leads me back into the dressing room. It's a lot more crowded than it was the day I got hired. Some of the girls don't even acknowledge me, some offer me a small smile, some scowl in my direction, and one comes running excitedly.

"Oh my God! New girl, I'm Taylor. We're going to have so much fun!"

Taylor wraps her arms around me and hugs me tight. Taylor is a beautiful short brunette who has the curves I wish I had. She's in a tiny pleated skirt and a white bikini top that can barely contain her breasts. Her hair is in pigtails.

"Hi, I'm Carrington."

Her smile and energy are contagious, and I think this could be a good friendship.

Bridgette says she'll see us out front in a little bit. I grab my bag and stand in front of the mirror. The whole time I'm making my eyes smoky and my cheeks dewy, Taylor is talking my ear off. She's a single mom to a six-year-old boy who is her reason for living. Taylor says she works at the Thirsty Beaver because what she makes here in only three days a week takes five days a week at other clubs.

After finishing my makeup, Taylor helps me copy her hairstyle. I grab my uniform out of my locker. It's a black G-string with a tiny black pleated skirt and a red bikini top. Taylor helps me finish the look with a white collar that velcros around my neck and looks like the top of a button-up shirt. A tiny red and black checkered tie hangs to the top of my breasts. On each wrist is a white wristband that looks like the cuff of the same button-up shirt.

It's definitely the naughty schoolgirl look. I slip into my black heels, which are not like the typical stripper shoes, the ones with the huge platforms and big heels. I just cannot wear them because I keep falling over in them. These heels I'm wearing now are five-inch spiked heels with no platform. Hopefully they'll work. I'm happy to see that Taylor has the same type of shoes.

"You look great! Are you nervous?" Taylor asks

as she grabs my arm and walks me toward the door that leads out to the main area.

"Not nervous, just not sure what to expect."

"Oh, you have nothing to worry about. Rafe and Tucker have top-notch security here. Damien and his team are vigilant. They don't let the customers get too handsy. Plus, they're not too hard on the eyes, if you like the bad boy type."

She winks at me as we step onto the floor and look for Bridgette. The statuesque blonde is standing by the bar. She waves us over and shares her expectations with us. Taylor promises her that she'll get me all trained. We watch her walk away. I want to ask Taylor about Bridgette. Does Bridgette look at the other women like she does her? I don't dare. What if Taylor went right to the other woman and told her I was asking? Maybe some other time.

Taylor introduces me to the bartenders, Kyle and Chet. Both men seem nice and more interested in each other than anyone else. We grab our trays, and when I turn around I freeze because the most beautiful man I've ever seen just walked in the door.

Chapter Two

Damien

Very slowly, I slide out of the bed and grab my jeans off of the floor. I quickly pull them on, snag my t-shirt up off of the floor, and slide it back on. I sit down on the chair in the corner of the room while I throw my socks and boots on.

"Why are you leaving?" she asks, her voice husky. I met her last night at the bar by my house called the Rusty Nail. Her name is on the tip of my tongue, but I honestly can't remember what it is.

"Got shit to do."

I stand up and look at her. They all seem to run together. One girl, same as the next, but with my job it's what I'll take. Since I work undercover, I don't have time for relationships. It's never wise to start something with someone when everything you tell them is a lie. So a few nights a week, I go to a bar, pick up a girl, fuck at her place, and then go home.

"Will I see you again?"

"Probably not. See ya."

I get up and, without a backward glance, walk out of her apartment and to my motorcycle. She's probably pissed right now, but whenever I pick up a girl I make sure she knows the deal. It's sex and nothing more. They all agree until I start to leave.

Once I get back to my place, I crawl into my bed, but my phone rings. It's the phone that's for my parents only, so my guess is it's my mom.

"Hey, Mom. How's it going?"

"Hey, honey. We're good. I just wanted to check in with you and see how you're doing."

She knows I can't talk about my undercover work, so I give her my obligatory, "I'm fine."

"Well, son, your father and I would like you to join us for dinner when you're able."

My parents supported my decision one hundred percent when I joined the DEA. I come from a long line of law enforcement—my father, his brothers, and their father. It's in my blood, always has been. I was twenty-two when my best friend growing up died of a heroin overdose, and it pushed to me to become an agent.

I'm the perfect man for undercover work. I'm covered in tattoos, and I have gauges in my ears. I guess, to my boss, that means I look like the shady type.

"Mom, I promise you that as soon as I'm able, I'll come to dinner. I've got to let you go so I can get some sleep before work. Love you."

We hang up. With a pillow over my head, I go to sleep.

On my black Indian Chief Dark Horse, I pull into the parking lot of The Thirsty Beaver. When I was first given this assignment, I was convinced that being surrounded by all of that pussy was going to be brutal. I thought I'd be tempted to fuck all of them, but it wasn't hard at all. Sure, a lot of these girls are beautiful and have smoking hot bodies, but they are bitches, straight up bitches.

Once they realized that I wasn't going to fuck any of them, they started getting attitude with me, but at least it didn't last long and now we just coexist. There are maybe a small handful of dancers and waitresses that I can stand, and those are the ones working there to make the money to move on to something better. I don't think that any of the girls realize that Rafe and Tucker are fucked up dudes. They've got their hands in all sorts of shit, and it's my job to find out what and who they're working for.

My job is to get into their inner circle and find out who their supplier is. After six months working here, I'm finally on my way to being someone they can trust. I back my bike into my spot and shut it off, staring at the building in front of me. With a sigh I climb off and head inside.

The place isn't filled up yet, but in a couple of hours it'll get crazy in here. Rafe and Tucker have definitely done a great job making a name for themselves, but I'm sure a lot of it has to do with all of the "extra services" the guys provide. I haven't figured out if they're pimping any of the girls yet, but so far I think they have a separate place for that.

I find Rafe and Tucker standing by the bar and make my way toward them. They're brothers, but they look nothing alike. Rafe is almost as tall as my six foot four self and lean with dark hair and even darker eyes that I swear look dead half the time. Tucker looks like a good ole' country boy, tall but not as tall as his brother and a little on the stockier side with light brown hair and blue eyes. I've run them both through the department database, and there is nothing on either of them.

My guess is their names are just aliases, or worse they're just that good and haven't been caught…yet.

"Damien, what's up, brother?"

I give them a chin lift. "Not much. Anything I need to know for tonight?"

Me and my security team monitor this place closely. The girls' safety is our top priority. The only time they're left alone are during private dances, but we're right outside the room.

"We've got a bachelor party coming in at eleven, but other than that it shouldn't be too crazy. We've got a new cocktail waitress who started tonight. Keep an eye on her. She's fucking hot and the guys are going to eat her up," Rafe says and then looks behind me. "There she is now. She's the redhead with Taylor."

Tucker wolf whistles when he looks to where his brother is looking. My curiosity is peaked as I turn around and check out this new girl. My eyes travel up long tanned legs, a flat stomach, a pierced belly button, perky tits, and a gorgeous face. I'm frozen where I stand. That girl has trouble written all over

15

her, and not the bad kind of trouble, the best kind. She needs to get gone. These animals will eat her alive.

My feet carry me toward her, and I can tell I'm intimidating her because she's all wide-eyed as she stares at me. The closer I get, I can see she's got that girl next door look under all of that makeup. She has a light smattering of freckles across the bridge of her nose and the apples of her cheeks.

"Hi, Damien! This is Carrington. Today's her first day," Taylor says happily. She's one of the few that I actually like. She's a sweet kid just trying to do right by her son.

"Hey, Taylor." I look at Carrington. "New girl, make sure you're fast or these guys will eat you alive."

I turn on my heel and walk across the room, to the other side. I feel her eyes on me, but I won't give in and turn toward her. She makes me think all sorts of nasty thoughts. I'm just going to have to be a dick to her so she stays away from me. She's a temptation I don't need right now.

All night long, I watch her move through the tables with Taylor, and just as I expected, the guys are hanging all over her. I hang around close to the floor to make sure no one crosses the line with the girls. I glance at the bar and see Rafe signaling for me to come to him.

"What's up?" I ask.

"We've been talking, and Tuck and I would like to give you more responsibility if you're up for it. You've proven your loyalty to us over and over, and we could really use someone with your skill set.

Give us a couple of weeks to put stuff together and we'll bring you in." Rafe looks at me like he's offering me the world, like I should be grateful.

I give him a nod. "That's great. I'm more than willing to take on more responsibility. Whenever you're ready, I'm ready."

"That's what we like to hear," Tucker says. "How's the new girl working out?"

"It's too soon to tell, but I don't think she's going to hack it."

All three of us turn to watch her. Carrington's standing at a table full of preppy little shitheads. I don't like the way they're staring at her, but I won't make a move unless they cross a line.

"She seems to be doing fine to me," Rafe says as he moves to stand next to me. "What do you think my chances are with her?"

"Haven't you learned yet that you shouldn't fuck the help? You're just setting yourself up for trouble. I'd stay away from her. Remember what happened when you were fucking Candy?"

About three months ago, he fucked one of our ex-dancers, and her boyfriend showed up and started tearing up the place. It was the first time since I went undercover there that I had to prove my loyalty, so I took the guy out back and, while a couple of the security guards held him, I hit him over and over again until finally the guy collapsed.

I took no pleasure in beating the guy's ass, but it earned me some respect from Rafe and Tucker, which was the goal from the beginning.

The rest of the night is pretty relaxed. The crowd is well-behaved. Every now and then, I'd let my eyes drift to Carrington, who seemed to be holding her own because Taylor was working one side while Carrington took care of the other. I don't want to admit that Carrington is doing a great job, but she is.

The girls all cash out and head back to the dressing room at the end of the night. We have a crew that comes in to clean after we close. That way, when the girls are done, they can just go home. I will admit that, for as much bad shit that Rafe and Tucker are into, they really take care of their girls. Another guy on my security team and I always hang around so we can escort the ladies out to their cars and make sure no drunk assholes are hanging around to bother any of the girls.

Ryan, who is from my team, escorts the majority of the girls out. When I hear laughter coming from the hallway, I turn to see Taylor and Carrington walking out. Carrington looked hot in the uniform, but now, in cut offs, an off-the-shoulder t-shirt, and flip-flops she looks fucking sexy. My cock is getting hard just looking at her.

"New girl!" I bark out. She freezes in place with Taylor standing next to her. "Bye, Taylor." The curvy brunette takes the hint and heads out.

I move until I'm standing in front of Carrington. I'm a big guy and I tower over her, but she stiffens her spine and scowls up at me.

"If you're going to make it here, you're going to have to be faster."

It's a fucking lame excuse to berate her, but I'm grasping at any excuse I can to ride her ass. Great, now my cock is getting hard again thinking about riding her.

"Um, okay. I thought I was doing okay for my first night, but tomorrow I'll be faster."

I can see her eyes flare, and she stands up a little taller. I've always been able to read people, and she wants to chew me out, I can tell. If she doesn't unclench her jaw, I'll start to hear teeth shatter.

"Well, make sure that you do."

On silent feet, I follow her out to the parking lot and watch her climb into a black Corolla. She backs out of her spot and drives past me, and I swear to God she just flipped me off. I look at her license plate and memorize it before heading back inside.

Chapter Three

Carrington

I've been working at The Thirsty Beaver for a month, and it's been going well. Sure, I'm exhausted from working there three nights and then working at least two nights a week in the ER, but the money is great. I already set aside the money to retake my boards and have even started a savings account.

Even with all of the good stuff, there is one bad thing, or I should say bad person. Damien. I don't know what his beef with me is, but every fucking time we work together, he rides my ass about everything. I swear, sometimes I'm so close to taking off my heels and stabbing him in the face with them, which sucks because he's fucking gorgeous in that total bad boy, I'm-gonna-break-your-heart way. Too bad the guy is a prick. Well, at least to me he is.

Last night Taylor pulled me back into the dressing room after Damien told me I should do something with myself because I wasn't sexy enough. For some reason, those words cut me deep and really fucking hurt. I'm glad she took me to the dressing room because I wasn't going to let that hot asshole see me cry.

"Honey, what happened? What did he say to you?" Taylor asks as she holds my hands in hers.

"He told me I wasn't sexy enough. I don't know what I did to him, but he hates me." I squeeze my eyes shut. "Taylor, every night he rides me about every thing." I look at the floor as I tell her about him bitching because I'm "too slow" or I'm "screwing up orders." It doesn't matter what I do because to him, I did it wrong.

"That's crazy. He's always been such a nice guy to the rest of us. I think you're doing great. The customers love you, and you interact great with them. I don't know what his issue is, but don't let him bother you," Taylor said before leaving me alone to get myself together. Then she headed back out there.

My breath left me in a whoosh before I grabbed the handle of the door, pulling it open to head back onto the floor.

My mind shifts back to the present. As I drive toward the diner by the dance studio on Main Street, I can't help but wonder what my dad needs to talk to me about. I wasn't surprised when he called me and "requested" my presence at lunch, because over the past two weeks I've hardly talked to them. Between both jobs, I'm exhausted, and honestly if I'm not at work, I'm home, sleeping. Abby and I have barely seen each other since she's started sort of talking to the hot deputy.

I park my car in front of the dance studio and walk down the brick sidewalk toward Sam's diner. Up ahead I see my dad leaning against his truck, typing on his phone. My dad is so handsome, especially for a guy in his early fifties. His blond hair is mostly gray, but it's a pretty gray. Somehow the tiny lines around his eyes really show off the green of them. He's still in great shape. My mom, who's a personal trainer, works him out.

"Hey, old man," I call out. He pushes away from his truck as I run toward him.

"Hi, my beautiful girl. I've missed you." He wraps me in a bear hug, squeezing me tight against his chest. "You feel thinner. Are you eating?" He lets go of me and wraps an arm around my shoulders as we make our way to the diner.

"I'm eating, Daddy. I've just been working a lot lately, and I'm still trying to get used to working third shift. My days still get all screwy."

A waitress seats us in a booth, and we both order iced tea before she leaves us.

"How is it being a nurse? You know, your mom and I are so proud of you. You worked so hard to get where you are."

Oh God, I hate lying to my dad. "It's going good. I'm learning a lot." I keep it brief, which I know is going to set off red flags with my dad. I usually don't ever stop talking. "How's Wukey?"

Both my dad and my brother share the same name, Luke. My parents said I've been calling him Wukey since he was born and I couldn't say my L's correctly, and it just kind of stuck.

22

"He's doing good. Just busy getting ready for graduation. His coach from LSU wants him there after the fourth of July to start training." My brother got recruited and offered a full scholarship from Louisiana State to play baseball and plans on studying construction management. I'm sure he'll start interning at our dad's and uncle's construction and restoration company during the summers, when he's not training.

"How's Mom going to handle having her baby boy gone?" Sarcasm laces my voice. I swear my baby brother can do no wrong in their eyes. Ugh, I hate when I sound whiney, even if it's in my own head.

My dad's hand shoots across the table and grabs mine. "Hey, your mom misses you a lot. Why don't you call her? She'd love to hear from you. She would've been here too, but she had a client and they couldn't reschedule."

When I was younger, my mom and I were really close, but then when I was around ten I noticed that my mom went into this weird sort of depression, even though I didn't know what depression was. It was always on February eleventh, and my grandma and grandpa Carter, or grandma and grandpa Carmichael, would pick me and my brother up and keep us for the day. We'd get home and there was always this heaviness in the air, and Dad would ask for us to be quiet and good. He'd disappear into their room, occasionally coming out to check on us, but then he'd go right back into their room with Mom.

My grandparents would sometimes stop by and

go into my parents' bedroom to see Mom and then come out to visit with us. It was when I was around thirteen or fourteen that Mom and Dad sat me down and explained that I had a sister who died while still in my mom's stomach. I saw how upset my mom got talking about it and, in that moment, I realized that I was simply a replacement child for the one they lost.

I've never told them I felt that. Instead, I became the wild child, doing my own thing and not caring what anyone thought.

"Care bear?" My dad squeezes my hand and pulls me out of my thoughts. "What's going on with you?"

"Nothing, Daddy. I'm just tired."

The rest of our lunch, we keep the conversation light, and I realize that I do need to call my mom. When we finish, he leads me outside and we stop by his truck.

"Don't be a stranger, and call your mother."

I wrap my arms around his middle. "I will. I love you, Dad."

"I love you too, sweetheart." I stand on the sidewalk and watch him climb in his truck and then drive away.

"Was that your dad?"

I scream. I turn around to find the asshole, Damien, standing behind me and again looking at me like I'm an idiot.

"Nope, that was my lover." In a huff I turn and start walking away, but he stops me with a hand on my arm.

"Whatever, smartass. I heard you call him dad."

24

His lip curls in a smirk, but I will not be turned on by it because he's a jerk.

"Well, this was fun. See you later," I say before turning away from him and walking as fast as I can down the street to my car. With a quick glance, I look behind me and find Damien still standing down the street, looking at me. Aviator sunglasses shield his eyes, so I can't see them. A girl in a tiny little skirt and tank top appears out of nowhere, wrapping her arms around Damien. I should look away, I shouldn't care, but my stomach clenches as I watch his hand slide down her back until it settles on her ass.

With a shake of my head, I climb inside my car and head home to take a nap. I work tonight, so I want to make sure I'm well-rested. When I pull into the parking lot of my apartment complex, I see that Abby's gone and feel a little bummed. I was hoping to get the scoop on the guy she's dating. I know they're spending a lot of time together and are getting really serious. I've seen him in passing, but I haven't had the chance to formally meet him yet. All I know is that he's a babe and Abby is one lucky girl.

I walk up the sidewalk, toward our door. The fragrant scent of the flowers that line the walkway wrap around me. I have no green thumb, so I don't know what type of flowers they are, but they're a beautiful mixture of deep purples and vibrant whites.

I make my way inside our apartment and head straight to my room. I'm on edge, and I know what I need to calm me down. My clothes hit the floor as

I strip naked and then crawl into my bed. I grab my vibrator out of the drawer in my nightstand. With my purple monstrosity in my hand, I lie flat on my back and close my eyes. I'm really good at conjuring up fantasies in my head. Of course my stupid brain picks Damien.

We're the only two at the club. He's been his usual asshole self to me, but tonight it's got me hot and bothered and so wet. I bite my lip as he walks toward me with that arrogant swagger of his. My pussy convulses as he looks me up and down and then very slowly licks his lips. An involuntary moan escapes my lips at his actions.

When he's right in front of me, he whispers, "Play with your nipples."

I pinch and roll them between my fingers. I can feel myself getting wet as I continue to play with them.

I moan as he tells me to slide my hand down my body to my pussy. My fingers slide through my wet pussy, and I grab my vibrator, turning it on. *His lips finally touch my neck, and I cry out as his teeth grab onto the skin of my neck.*

He picks me up and sets my ass on the stage. "Don't move." His voice is low. I do as he says and hold still.

His lips travel between my breasts and down my stomach until he reaches the apex of my thighs. He spreads my legs and uses his thumbs to open me. His breath tickles me as he leans in close. "I need to taste you before I fuck you." His tongue swipes up and down, once then twice.

I cry out, gripping his head with my hands. He pulls away from my pussy, and I cry out in frustration, but that quickly turns to a moan when Damien unzips his jeans and pulls his long, thick dick out of his pants. He moves closer, and then he's thrusting inside me. My back arches off the stage as he leans forward, sucking a nipple into his mouth.

I've never felt so full in my life. He's stretching me so much, it hurts, but it hurts so good. He hammers into me over and over.

"Fuck me harder, baby," I moan out. The telltale sign that I'm going to come starts in my belly. My hips drive up to meet his thrusts as his groans get louder, vibrating against my skin.

"Are you going to come for me, baby?"

He pinches my clit, and I explode around him. I feel my walls clamp down on him as I begin to feel him pulse inside of me. He slows his strokes, kissing my lips softly.

The buzzing of my vibrator pulls me from my fantasy. I toss it to the side and lie there, catching my breath. Ugh…Now I'm going to think about that stupid fantasy every time I see him. I'm just not going to worry about it or him. He's got a woman, and I shouldn't be surprised because he is a gorgeous man.

I throw on my robe, wash my vibrator, and then crawl under the covers.

Chapter Four

Damien

It's been two weeks since the day I ran into Carrington on Main Street. I'll never admit to anyone that when I first saw her with her dad, I thought he might be her boyfriend, and it caused something to knot in my belly, which I could only describe as pure jealousy. The way she smiled at her dad was a smile I'd love to have directed at me, but fuck, it can't happen. Corrine meeting me for lunch was just what I needed to push Carrington away.

Corrine is everything that Carrington doesn't seem to be: big breasted—fake, of course— bleached hair, too skinny, and dumb as fuck. Corrine served a purpose. She was an easy lay and wasn't clingy, so when she came to me on the sidewalk I grabbed onto her, laying it on thick, because I knew Carrington was watching.

It worked, because since that day she won't even look at me, and picking on her just gets me an eye roll. I'm never too far from her, and I always find ways to learn about her. I know it's bordering on stalkerish, but I'm just drawn to her. It's like a sickness. Taylor has been the perfect person to find out stuff. From Taylor, I learned that Carrington has a younger brother and went to nursing school but failed her boards. That's why she's working here, to make money to retake them and to keep being able to pay her bills. She lives with her cousin, who is also her best friend. See, she's turning me into a fucking stalker.

Now I'm at the bar with Rafe and Tucker. "Hang out tonight after we close up. We want to run some stuff by you." This comes from Rafe. Finally, I'm getting brought in to their inner circle. I'll finally start figuring out what the fuck they're doing.

That right there is the reason I'd never get involved with any of the girls that work here. I don't know who's doing what. Of course, my eyes immediately seek *her* out. I find her on the other side of the club with her arm slung around Taylor's shoulders, laughing at something Taylor is saying to her. I have to force myself to stay where I am even though the sound of her laughter is trying to entrance me, but I won't let it—I can't.

Bridgette rushes over to us. "Stephanie didn't show up tonight. We're short a dancer. I want to ask Carrington. Can I?"

I want to tell her hell no, but I remain silent. "Do it," Rafe says. "She's got one shot. If she fucks it up, she's back to serving drinks." He turns to me. "We'll talk later."

Bridgette moves across the room and whispers to Carrington. I'm hoping she tells the other woman

Evan Grace

no, but instead she nods at her. She runs outside and returns minutes later. She goes to the DJ booth, hands him a CD, and then runs to the dressing room. This is either going to go really well or really bad.

***

The club is packed, and the crowd is on the rowdy side. I've already had to kick out one group after I repeatedly told them not to grab the waitresses and pull them into their laps. Taylor, who is one of the happiest people I've ever met, was starting to get pissy about it. Things have been a little better since they left.

Dancer after dancer gets up on the stage and does their thing. It's sad when you become desensitized to beautiful women dancing almost completely naked, but when you see it all the time, it loses its allure really quick.

"Gentleman, we have a special treat for you tonight!" the DJ calls out over the speakers. "Our girl Pepper is making her dancing debut. Show her some love."

Pepper? I think to myself. What kind of stage name is that? I don't get to think too much about it because the music starts and there she is. Fuuuck me, I don't know what the song is, but it's got a slower beat. Her hips sway as she struts her way toward the front of the stage. She's wearing her hair in big loose curls that hang down her back. Her outfit is the little black skirt that's part of her uniform and barely covers her ass, and the top is a

30

thin white tank top that is tied right under her breasts.

She certainly knows what she's doing as she shakes her hips. I watch her move toward the pole and grab it and then start twirling around it like she's done it a thousand times. The guys in the crowd go crazy. I signal my other security guys, making sure they stay close just in case.

After twirling around the pole, she turns her back to the crowd and slowly works her hips. The skirt she's wearing slides down her legs until she steps out of it to reveal a tiny black G-string and a gorgeous ass. My dick immediately gets hard. She rubs her hands seductively over her body. As the next song plays, she does some more spins around the poles and crawls across the stage, where the men are all but throwing money at her.

On her knees at the end of the stage, Carrington grabs her shirt with both hands and pulls. It rips right down the middle. The guys all start clapping and whistling, and I make my move toward the stage. When the music ends she moves around the stage, collecting the money. Me and one of my guys, Tim, move toward the stairs to keep anyone from trying to grab at her as she steps off the stage. She doesn't even look at me when she steps down.

It's not until she disappears down the hallway toward the dressing room that I realize she never opened her shirt after she ripped it open. What a tease.

***

Carrington

Dancing was a lot easier than I thought it would be. Last Saturday, after the first dance, it got easier, and when the moment came that I had to take my top off I just imagined I was at home, alone dancing in my room. Wearing pasties kind of helped. They made me feel a little less naked up top. By the time the night was over, I had made three hundred dollars in tips.

Taylor sat with me for a little while after the club closed. The adrenaline had still been pumping though my veins. When I asked Taylor why she never danced, she told me that she had two left feet. While I was up on stage I felt the dickhead's eyes on me, and in a way I felt like I was dancing for him.

This morning I was surprised when Bridgette called me and asked me to come in. She said she wanted to talk to me about Saturday night. I wonder if I did something wrong, or maybe they didn't like it.

Since I'm off today, I hope Bridgette won't be bothered that I'm in bumming around clothes: cotton shorts, tank top, and flip-flops. I didn't even bother with makeup today. I pull into the parking lot and see that there are two cars and one motorcycle. When I get out and reach the door, Tucker, who I talked to a little bit on Saturday, opens the door for me.

"Hey, beautiful." I smile and shake my head as I walk past him.

"Hi, handsome," I say with a wink.

I walk down the hall to the double doors. He opens it for me, and I step inside to find Bridgette waiting for me. My pulse picks up speed as I walk toward her. Did I dance that terribly? I thought it went well. Doubts plague me as I stop in front of her.

"Hi," I say, keeping my voice steady.

"Let's go talk in my office." I follow her through the club and down the hall to her office. "Sit," she tells me.

My knee bounces up and down as I wait for her to sit. I really don't want to have to beg for my job back at the hospital. "So, I wanted to bring you in to talk about your future here. Saturday night you put on one hell of a show. It was very sexy, and the men all went crazy for you. I've been talking to Rafe and Tucker, and we want to make you the main attraction."

I'm speechless. "Um, are you serious? I thought you were going to tell me it was terrible. What do you mean by main attraction?"

Bridgette leans back in her chair and crosses one leg over the other. "You could make us a lot of money. You're sexy with a hint of girl next door. We want you dancing three times a night, Friday and Saturday's only. You've had dance training, yes?"

"Um, yeah. I've been dancing for a while, and I've been trained in many styles. I even took a burlesque workshop and an exotic dance workshop too."

"We're thinking costumes and possibly props. We've been looking into changing things up a bit for a while now, so this is the perfect opportunity. We'll be bringing the others in over the next couple of days to tell them about the change."

There's a knock on the door, and we both turn toward it. Damien steps inside, looking hot as hell.

I turn away from him and look at Bridgette. He's been nothing but an asshole to me.

"Rafe needs you quick." His voice is slightly hoarse. It almost sounds like he has just woken up.

"I'll be right back."

I watch Bridgette get up and leave the office. I expect Damien to follow her, but instead he closes and locks the door behind him. I pop up out of my chair as he stalks toward me. I move around the desk and back up until my back meets the wall. He doesn't stop until his chest brushes mine and his arms cage me in.

"I don't want you dancing," he growls.

I'm stunned at first. He's never had a problem showing his distaste for me, but this is the first time he's been…ugh, I don't even know how to describe it, but enough is enough. I stand as tall as I can, showing him he doesn't intimidate me. I poke him in the chest with my finger.

"You know what? I don't give a shit what you want. I don't know what I did to you, but you've done nothing but treat me like shit since I started working here. I'm a good person, I'm nice, I don't treat people bad, but right now I want to kick you in the fucking balls."

I try to shove him away from me, but he's an unmovable mountain of a man. He pulls me to him, wraps an arm around me, and grabs a handful of my hair, using it to tip my head back.

I'd never admit it to him, but it makes me a little wet. In seconds, his mouth is on mine. I'm shocked at first, but then I can't help it and begin kissing him back. His lips are full and soft as they devour mine. He lets go of my hair, and then I'm up in the air with my legs wrapped around his waist. He licks at the seam of my lips until I open to him and let my tongue brush against his.

His dick is hard and rubs against the apex of my thighs, and I moan against his mouth. I'm so wet that the simplest touch to my clit and I'll explode, but just as quickly as the kiss started, it ends, and the door slams shut behind him. I lean against the wall to stop myself from falling because my legs feel like jelly.

Once the horny haze wears off, I take a deep breath and sit back down in my seat so I can wait for Bridgette.

Chapter Five

Damien

It's been a month since I kissed Cari, and I can't stop fucking thinking about her. The way her lips molded perfectly to mine, the way her pupils dilated when I grabbed her hair by the base of her skull, and the way it felt grinding against her when I had her against the wall. I've tried fucking other women, but that quit working, so I've conjured some grade-A fantasies and use my hand, jerking off almost every night like I'm a goddamn teenager again.

On a positive note, I've finally situated myself right where I wanted to be, in Rafe and Tucker's circle of "friends." My mission is to get in close with them and gather useful information to begin the process of bringing them down. So far, they've had me deliver thick envelopes to a couple of different guys, and I've memorized their information so I can give it to my handler. Unfortunately they're just low level dealers, but they'll be watched to see if they come in contact with Rafe and Tucker's main supplier. It's become quite clear that they're working for someone with a lot more power, but who? That's the question I need answered.

The cellphone that my parents have the number to rings, and I grab it off my nightstand. "Hey, Mom."

"Happy birthday, my baby boy!" she sings, and I can't help but smile. My mom and baby sister, Victoria, have always made a big deal out of birthdays in our house when I was growing up. It certainly never slowed down after I moved out.

"Thanks, Mom. How're you doing?"

"We're good, baby. Your sister sends her love and so does your father. Do you think you might be able to come over tomorrow for dinner? I know you're working, but I just had to ask."

I know my mom hates that I work undercover, but she respects that this is what I want to do. Bringing down scum like Rafe and Tucker and the scumbags they work for is my mission.

"I should be able to swing that." If I go see my parents, I have to take precautions to make sure I'm not being followed.

"That's great! Come around six and let me know if anything comes up and you can't come."

I tell her I'll be there, but yes, I'll call if things change.

I jump in the shower and then get ready for work. I throw on a black t-shirt, jeans, and my black motorcycle boots. I throw a little gel in my hair and run my fingers through it until it's styled how I want it. I put my wallet into my back pocket and grab my helmet since I'm riding my bike to the club.

Fall is right around the corner. It's starting to get cooler at night. I'm looking forward to finally being done with this case, sooner rather than later so I can hop on my bike and ride up the coast. I pull into the parking lot and back my bike into my parking spot.

Taylor is behind the bar when I step inside. She takes my helmet for me and sticks it under the bar.

"Thanks," I tell her, and she hands me a bottle of water.

"Sure thing! Happy birthday, by the way."

I'm not sure how she knew it was my birthday, but I just give her a chin lift and then make my way back to Rafe and Tucker's office. I knock and wait for one of them to answer, but it's Bridgette that opens the door.

"Come on in." She shuts the door behind me. Rafe and Tucker stand up, and we exchange the obligatory half handshake, back slap hug. I sit on the sofa on one end while Rafe sits on the other end.

"What's going on?" I ask.

"We're on our way to becoming the top gentleman's club in South Carolina, and we have Carrington to thank for that. Our numbers are up one hundred percent. We have a line to get in every night. Liquor sales are through the roof. The general consensus is that guys like coming here because it's not like any other club." I don't like the look on his face. "We want to step it up a notch. The private rooms in back could become a huge moneymaker for us. We're thinking about starting to throw private parties in those rooms."

My facial expression stays impassive as I listen to them tell me about their plan to start renting out those rooms nightly to big spenders. We'll provide everything for them—drugs, booze, and pussy. The girls will get a cut of the profits, and Rafe and Tucker will either take volunteers to work the rooms or bring in girls.

I knew they were gearing up for something, but I had no clue what. They've been so tight-lipped about stuff, but now they're letting me in.

"Do you want me to start asking the girls?" I ask.

"No. Thanks, but Bridgette's going to handle that," Tucker says. "We've already asked Taylor, but she turned us down."

I silently pray that they don't ask Cari. She doesn't seem like the type to sleep with men for money, but I guess you can never tell.

"Happy birthday, by the way," Rafe says, and they hand me an envelope.

"What's this?" I take it from him and look inside to find a nice stack of one hundred dollar bills. "Thanks, but I don't understand."

"The past seven or so months you've been here, you've become an important part of our business, and we just wanted to thank you for everything that you've done for us."

I'll take the money, but I won't be spending any of it. It's probably dirty, so I'll turn this in to my handler. He can see if it can be traced.

"Thanks again for this. I appreciate it. I better get out there and see what's going on."

I get up and make my way back out onto the

floor. I find Carrington standing at the bar with Taylor. Her hair is piled up on top of her head. A pink hoody covers her top, and she's wearing those damn cut-off jean shorts that show off her legs, which seem even leaner since she started dancing here.

She turns toward me when Taylor waves at me, but as soon as she sees me, she turns back around. It's obvious she's still upset about that day last month. She seems tense. I know something is going on with her family, and that's only because, again, I've turned into a damn stalker when it comes to her.

I watch her hug Taylor and then take off down the hall, toward the dressing room.

"Oh my God! You totally like her!" I turn around and face Taylor, who's bouncing up and down on her toes.

"No, I don't. Taylor, you don't know what you're talking about."

"Just keep telling yourself that. I've seen you watch her. Anytime she's on stage or even in the same room as you, you watch her like a hawk. Take her out." She hugs me tight before turning to grab her tray off the bar.

She's crazy.

***

The night's been busy but manageable. There was only one guy that tried to grab for Cari, so I got the extreme pleasure of tossing his ass outside. Since they changed up the girls' routines, it's a lot more entertaining watching them dance. The guys in the crowd all love it. Therefore, the money has been rolling in.

We're all benefiting from the new popularity of the club. Before I head to my parents' place tomorrow, I need to meet with my handler and let him know that the brothers are looking to expand their business.

I turn back toward the stage and find Rafe standing on it with a microphone in his hand. What the fuck is he doing?

"Good evening, gentlemen. We'll have our gorgeous dancers back out for you again in a bit, but first we want to recognize a certain head of security. You all know Damien. Well, today's his birthday. Come up here for a minute." With reluctant steps, I make my way up on the stage. "I've got a special treat for you, brother. Here, have a seat." I sit down in the chair that's on the stage. "Our very own Pepper is going to give you a birthday lap dance. Who wants to see Pepper do it?"

The crowd roars as she comes walking through the crowd and up onto the stage. She looks about as uncomfortable as I feel.

The music starts and she undoes her robe, letting it fall to the floor. I try to school my features, but it's hard because she's so fucking hot in her little royal blue bikini and heels. On her hands and knees, she slowly crawls toward me, and once she reaches my legs, she grabs my knees and pulls them apart. My cock immediately gets hard as she slides between my legs, grabs on to my shoulders, and lets her body slide up mine, never taking her eyes off of mine.

When she's standing up to her full height, I want desperately to grab and touch every inch of her, but with quick movements she's behind me. She runs her hands down my chest and drags her nails up my chest, and I swear to God she licks my ear. Cari moves around so she's in front of me again and straddles my lap. She starts rolling her hips, and my cock is trying to punch a hole through my jeans.

She grabs my hands and wraps them around her until my hands are filled with her ass cheeks. Even in the dim lights, I see her pupils dilate as she grinds against me. With my hands still on her, she arches her back and then lifts herself back up so she's looking at me. I swear for a minute her body tenses, but just as quickly she relaxes.

The song ends, and neither one of us moves as we stare at each other. God, I want to fuck her so bad right now. She's biting her bottom lip, but I want to be the one biting it. Damn Rafe and this fucking dance.

I finally move my hands from her ass, and she slowly stands up and grabs her robe. She wraps it around herself and then takes off down the stairs. The crowd cheers as they watch her walk by with Matt, one of the men on my security team, following closely behind her.

I look down at my lap to see if it's obvious that my dick's hard, and that's when I see it. She left a wet spot on the crotch of my jeans and I'm shocked. "Oh fuck," I whisper to myself. Rafe joins me on the stage, claps me on the back, and asks the crowd to give me a round of applause one more time before I grab the chair and make my way off of the stage.

"You're a lucky motherfucker!" some random asshole says to me as I walk by.

A couple of other guys stop me, and it takes all I have not to throttle them when they start talking about wanting to bang her.

It's when I reach the bar and throw back a shot that I decide that Cari and I are going to talk after work.

"What did you do to Carrington?" Taylor is scowling at me.

"I don't know what the fuck you're talking about. She was the one that was giving me the lap dance. Where is she?" I ask.

"She left, and she was acting weird," Taylor says. "Maybe I should go check on her."

"No, stay here. I'll go," I tell her, and I make my way to Bridgette's office.

Bridgette opens the door. She's partially dressed, and there's some douche bag sprawled out on the couch with no shirt on. I ask her for Carrington's address, giving her a bullshit excuse that I need to take her something.

I hop on my bike and pull out of the parking lot.

Chapter Six

Carrington

I step out of my shower and dry off then stare at myself in the mirror. I'm disgusted with myself. I had an orgasm in the middle of the club giving the one person who hates me a lap dance. The minute I placed his hands on my ass, I felt a tingling sensation all the way to my clit, and the moment I came in contact with his hard cock I couldn't stop myself from grinding against it and wishing it was inside of me, like I was some whore.

I take my hair down once I'm dried off and throw on my nightgown, and then I walk out to the kitchen to get a glass of wine. I really wish Abby was here, but she's at Ben's tonight. Since I've started dancing I've got about a thousand dollars saved, so maybe I should quit and just go back to the hospital full-time. It's clear I need to get away from Damien. All I seem to do is piss him off.

I slam back my glass of wine and pour one more when there's a knock on my door. It makes me nervous because it's one o'clock in the morning.

"Cari, open the door." Damien's voice carries through it.

Making my way toward the door, I freeze in front of it. Do I open it and feel his wrath or do I ignore him and hope that he goes away? I grab the doorknob and take a deep breath. I flip the deadbolts, and before I can even open the door it's flying open. Damien grabs me under the arms and lifts me. My legs automatically wrap around his waist. His lips are on mine so hard, I swear I can taste blood.

I wrap my arms around his shoulders as I grind against him. He moans against my mouth, using my wall to hold me up as he lets go of me to grab my nightgown and rip it open. Damien lifts me high so he can suck a nipple into his mouth. My cries echo through my apartment as he lavishes it with attention, causing it to stiffen. He bites at my sensitive flesh.

My hips move against him. Can he tell that I'm not wearing any panties? He switches to the other nipple and gives it the same treatment. I sift through his hair, gripping it tight and causing him to growl against my breast. He bites at the flesh at the top of my boob and begins to suck, marking me. I should stop him. How would I be able to cover it? But right now I don't care.

"Yes," I moan.

Damien's hands slide down until they're under my nightgown, and I know the exact moment he feels my bare pussy because his body tenses and then he slides one finger inside of me. My head flies

45

back and hits the wall with a thunk as he pumps it in and out of me. Every time he taps my magic spot deep inside my tight channel, I shudder around his digit, moaning.

"You're so wet, baby. Do you want my cock in your tight little pussy?" he breathes against my ear.

"God, yes. Please fuck me," I groan. I feel desperate and needy.

"Take me out."

My hands slide down between us, and I unbutton his pants. The sound of his zipper sliding down sounds loud in my apartment. I slide my hand inside, and when I connect with his cock my eyes widen as I look up at him. I've never in my entire life felt a cock this big. He's long and thick. Fuck, I don't think he's going to fit.

"Oh, I'll fit. You're going to love it," he says before nipping at my ear lobe and stroking that spot inside me relentlessly. "Oh fuck, baby. I can feel it coming. Give it to me."

I explode around him and feel the gush rush out of me. He groans against my skin, and before I can react he's sheathing himself and is at my opening. He presses in. In and out he begins to move, each time pressing in further and further. My eyes drift shut, but he growls at me to open them. His face is so close to mine that I reach out, cupping his cheek. I moan long and loud as he fills me full to bursting.

He holds my stare as he stays buried deep inside of me. Something is happening between us. I can't put it into words, but I can feel it. His eyes hold mine captive as he finally starts to move. With every deep thrust, my back hits the wall and I give him a half moan, half cry. I am so ready to come that it's starting to become painful. He tips my hips, which makes him hit me even deeper, if that's even possible. With his other hand, he reaches between us and uses his thumb to stroke my clit.

"Oh my God, oh shit!" I cry out just as I explode around him. I grab onto his shoulders, digging my nails into his flesh as my body tries to suck him in even deeper. He continues to pound into me as my orgasm threatens to consume me.

"I'm gonna come," he groans out as he thrusts once, twice. He holds himself deep on the third and leans forward, burying his face in my neck. He's still so deep inside me that I can feel each pulse of his cock as he comes.

His face stays buried in my neck as we both try to gain our composure. My heart is still pounding away in my chest, and my pussy feels like it's thumping in time with my heart around his cock. Damien's lips press against my neck, and it sends chills across my body.

I whimper as his softening cock slips out of me. With a gentleness that surprises me, he slowly helps me lower my feet to the floor. His hands slide into my hair, and he tips my head back. I bite my lip as I stare up at him. He's so large, and he towers over my five-foot-six frame. It makes me feel safe, treasured.

"You're so fucking beautiful. I tried to stay away from you, I swear to God I did." He presses his lips against my forehead and sighs.

After the both of us stood in my living room in awkward silence, he kisses my lips and asks me where the bathroom is. I point down the hall. "First door on the left."

"I'll be right back. Thanks, baby."

He disappears into the bathroom, and I look down at myself. The big rip in my nightgown exposes my breasts, and on one I've got a huge hickey. I shake my head and hold it closed.

Back in my room, I slide another nightgown over my head just as Damien steps out of the bathroom. On silent feet, he steps inside my bedroom and wraps his arms around me from behind. Now that my post-orgasmic fog has faded, I turn in his arms and stare up at him.

"What are you doing here? What was that?" Of course it's a little late to ask since I just had sex with him.

He reaches out again and tenderly strokes my cheek. "I told you. I tried to stay away from you. I've tried being a dick, I've tried using other girls, but you're all I've thought about." I don't know if I should be flattered or pissed that he slept with other girls instead of me. "I shouldn't be here," he says solemnly.

"Don't go." I push up on my toes and touch my lips to his. In seconds, he's got me up in his arms and then on my bed.

***

My eyes drift open, and last night starts replaying in my mind. I hadn't expected Damien to spend the night, but he did. When he stripped out of his shirt, I got to see his ink. It covered almost every inch of his upper body and arms. The tattoos were vibrant and beautifully done. He also had a piercing on each nipple. When we crawled into my bed, he pulled me to him. I rested my head on his shoulder, and he wrapped his arms around me, hugging me close.

We didn't talk. We both drifted to sleep. I don't know what time it was when he woke me up, but it was with his mouth on my neck. Slowly he worked me into a frenzy and then fucked me slow, so slow and oh so good. My orgasm wasn't explosive like earlier, but it was long and languid.

I slowly roll over. Damien's on his side, facing me. In sleep, he looks so relaxed, peaceful. At the club, he always looks like he's ready to fight. I reach out and trace the tattoo on his chest. That's one thing I've never really thought about doing. I've gotten my belly button pierced, but that's it. I'm not a big fan of needles. I trace around one of his nipple rings before moving across to the other.

I wiggle until we're chest to chest. I press my lips to his neck and slide my hand around his waist as I snuggle closer to him, breathing in his scent, woodsy with a hint of sweat. He wraps an arm around my waist and tangles his legs with mine.

"Go back to sleep, babe. It's too early," he mutters, his voice husky.

When his lips touch the top of my head, I swoon a little. I close my eyes and settle against him as my eyes drift shut.

***

My eyes flutter open, and I see that my bed is empty. Disappointment fills me, but I see a note on my nightstand under my phone. As soon as I pick it up, I unfold it and read.

Hey babe, I had shit to do today, but we should talk later. I'll stop by and see if you're home tonight.

Damien

I set the note back down and look at my phone. It's noon, and I'm running late for lunch with all the women in my family. I hop out of bed and quickly regret it. I feel like I've been beaten up. I cup myself between my legs. I'm freaking sore. Limping into the bathroom, I grab some ibuprofen and swallow them down. While I wait for them to kick in, I carefully step into the shower.

The hot water feels good beating down on my sore muscles. I've had great sex before, but last night he did things to my body, especially with that beautiful cock of his, that I've never experienced before. I've never been this sore afterward either, but it'll be a delicious reminder for me.

I climb out of the shower, feeling a lot better, and I run through my morning routine. My hair hangs down in loose waves, and my makeup is light. I decided on a maxi dress with a cardigan and jeweled sandals. Not my usual outfit, but I just feel like wearing something different.

Normally I'd wear a short skirt or shorts and a top that showed some skin, but maybe since I take off my clothes for a living now I just feel like keeping myself covered. I make my way toward The Waterfront, where my mom, grandma, aunts and cousins are all meeting for lunch. I'm looking forward to seeing everyone since it's been a while since I've seen them all.

Pulling into the parking lot, I hop out of my car and run toward the restaurant. I make my way inside and find the women in my family gathered around a long table.

"Hey, guys!"

I make my way around the table, hugging and kissing everyone. Abby has an empty chair next to her, so I sit down next to her. Her boyfriend's little girl, Natalie, is sitting in her lap.

"Hey, stranger, I've missed you!" Abby's pretty much been living with Ben, her boyfriend. Weird stuff has been happening to them. Abby has been getting prank calls, someone approached Ben's daughter at the park, and someone slashed Ben's tire.

She leans over and kisses my cheek. "I've missed you too."

"Hey, Natalie. You look so pretty today."

The little girl flashes me a bright smile. My mom looks across the table and gives me a sad smile, and I realize I haven't called her like Dad wanted me to. I feel horrible. I get up and move around the table.

"Hey, Mom. How are you?" I wrap my arms around her and kiss her cheek.

"Hi, baby. I feel like I haven't seen you in forever. How's the job going? Are they working you too hard?" My mom and I look a lot alike. Her hair has more brown than red, but I have the same blue eyes as her. She still has an amazing figure, which I know she works very hard at. She looks at my outfit and then back up at me. "You look beautiful, by the way."

"Thanks, Mom, and sorry. Work has kept me busy, but things are good, and no they're not working me too hard."

I make my way back to my seat while I feel a knot form in my belly. My brother does nothing wrong in their eyes while all my life they've been hard on me. Ugh, I shake my head. This isn't the time to feel sorry for myself.

After lunch and Abby's big announcement, we all say our goodbyes. I told Abby that I'd go pick up some bridal magazines and bring them over to Ben's so we can start planning. Stopping in Walgreen's, I grab a couple of different ones off the rack and then head toward Ben's place. The whole drive there, I think about last night with Damien and what he wants to talk about. I'm sure it'll be to tell me that he made a mistake, and then he'll go back to treating me like shit again.

When I pull into Ben's driveway and shut off my car, the hairs on the back of my neck stand up. Abby comes tearing out of the front door with Natalie in her arms, blood running down her face, and she's screaming. I scramble out of the car and run toward them, reaching for Natalie just as Abby goes down. Natalie clings to me, hysterically crying as I start screaming for help.

One of Ben's neighbors comes running across their yard. They've already called 911, and I can hear the sirens. I try to give Natalie to the woman that rushed over, but she won't let go of me. The police arrive first and disappear inside Ben's house. The paramedics and a fire truck show up right after.

In a flurry of activity, they put Abby on a stretcher and some man I've never seen on another. They tell me what hospital they're taking Abby to, and with Natalie in my arms I start making the dreadful calls.

***

Damien

I really hated leaving Carrington earlier today, but I had shit to do. A note wasn't probably the smartest move, but she was sleeping so peacefully and I didn't want to wake her. Before I left, I took the chance to check out her body more closely. She's a beautiful woman, and in sleep she looks like a red-headed angel. Her skin is satiny smooth. I knew she was probably sore today and I should've warned her, but I needed to be inside of her with an urgency that freaked me out.

Once I was buried deep inside her, it was like everything made sense, and fuck me, I liked it—I liked her. Tonight I'm going to tell her that last night was a mistake and it can't ever happen again. It's going to fucking blow, but for her safety it needs to happen. I can't tell her who I really am.

I pull down the alley of my parents' home and park my bike in their garage. With my helmet in my hand, I make my way toward the back door.

My mom opens it and greets me with a bright smile. "David, you're here!" She wraps her arms around me, hugging me close.

"Hey, Mom. You look good."

Two years ago, she had breast cancer and we almost lost her. Luckily, she's in remission. Her hair is still really short and is now completely gray, but she looks healthy. She's tiny and petite and looks a lot younger than my dad.

"Thank you, honey. Your dad is outside grilling the burgers, and Victoria's not going to be able to come because she's studying for finals."

She grabs me a beer, and I head out to my dad. "Hey, Dad, how's it going?"

"Hey, son. Happy birthday."

We ate out on the deck, and it was hard to find stuff to talk about since I couldn't talk about the case. Dad told me about fishing and golfing. Mom just hugs on me. After we finished eating our burgers, she brought out cherry pie, my favorite. My mom bought me a couple of new t-shirts and a new watch.

I didn't stay too late because I was beat and I wanted to get my talk with Carrington over with so I could go home and crash.

The night is starting to cool off as I head toward her apartment. I'm hoping this goes well, but I should probably be prepared for it to go bad. I pull into the parking lot and back my bike into a space in the visitor's section. With a deep breath, I make my way toward her apartment.

I'm almost to her door when I spot her. She's on the little balcony outside of her living room with her arms wrapped around her knees. I stop, watching her for a minute, and it hits me she's crying. Her shoulders are shaking, and her cries are almost silent.

I grab the bar and hoist myself over. "Carrington?" She startles and looks up at me, and that's when I see blood streaks on the front of her dress. Her eyes are puffy and glassy. Tears keep leaking from her eyes. "Baby, what happened?"

I get down on my haunches in front of her. She just keeps shaking her head back and forth. She moves slightly, but I see it's to grab a bottle of tequila. She holds it to her lips to take a healthy swallow. I reach out and grab the bottle from her and set it back down.

"Sweetheart, did someone hurt you?" She shakes her head. "Whose blood is that? Baby, you're scaring me. Tell me what's going on."

She flies out of her chair and wraps her arms around my neck as sobs wrack her body. I wind my arms around her, hugging her tight.

"M-My c-cousin was a-attacked today."

With her face in my neck, she tells me about her cousin Abby and how Abby was sexually assaulted and had attempted suicide a while ago. She tells me about how she went to Ben's house today just after a man attacked Abby in her fiancé's house.

"Is she okay?"

"Y-Yes. He broke her nose and slapped her around a little bit, but she'll be okay. I'm just glad that asshole is behind bars and before they locked him up she kicked his ass." She laughs a little against my neck, and damn, it causes my dick to twitch in my pants.

"Let's get you inside." I stand up and lead her inside, setting her on the sofa.

I grab a washcloth from her bathroom, get it wet, and bring it out with me. I sit down next to her and grab her face gently, turning it toward me. With gentle strokes, I wipe the makeup and tears from her face. She stares up at me with those big blue eyes of hers, and I just want to take the pain in them away. Carrington leans into my hand when I cup her cheek. She's killing me here. I came here to tell her we couldn't sleep together again, but dammit, I want to do whatever I can to take her pain away.

She must be able to read what I'm thinking, because she pushes me back and straddles my lap. Her lips tentatively move against mine until I grab her face and take over the kiss. Carrington's lips are soft against mine. The taste of tequila is on her lips. My tongue strokes the seam of her mouth, and she opens to me and starts stroking her tongue against mine.

This girl is going to be my downfall if I can't get control of myself. *Pull away*, I think to myself. *Get up and leave*, but I can't do it. Instead I let my hands drift up her thighs as I remove her dress. I grab her ass cheeks under her underwear, holding her tighter to me as I grind my hard dick against her. Her moans vibrate against my mouth.

I keep one hand on her ass and bring the other around, reaching inside her tiny silk panties, finding her swollen and wet. "Fuck, baby," I whisper against her lips as I start strumming her clit. Her moans drive me wild, and my dick is trying to bust through my jeans.

Carrington intertwines her fingers behind my neck while my fingers move swiftly over her clit until she whimpers and then cries out. I thrust two fingers inside of her, and a pleasured scream rips from her lips. Her sweet juices run down my finger, and her channel squeezes me.

I slow my movements and then stop when she leans against me and wraps her arms around me. As I kiss her temple, I pull my hand out of her panties and hold her stare as I suck one finger into my mouth, moaning when her taste explodes on my tongue. She's undoing my pants as I reach for a condom. This is what I'll do. I'll fuck her out of my system.

She takes it from my fingers and slowly rolls the latex down my length. I reach between us and hold my cock up as she moves over it and then slowly slides down my length. God, she's so fucking tight, and she has to work at getting me inside and buried deep, but when I get there she throws her head back with a long groan. I grab her hips and start rocking her back and forth. As I look down where we're connected, my dick pulses inside of her. Her pussy is stretched, but she's taking my entire dick like a champ.

I slide the straps of her dress down until they trap her arms at her sides. She isn't wearing a bra, so I wrap my lips around one turgid tip and bite down with enough pressure to hurt, but only a little. She's down for that. I can tell because she gets so wet. I suckle at her breast as she rides me and then switch sides, giving the other the same treatment.

Her cries are becoming more urgent, and she's starting to ride me faster so I reach up and pull her mouth to mine, swallowing her whimpers and cries. I grab her hips and start slamming her down on me over and over until she throws her head back with the most beautiful orgasmic cry I've ever heard. I pull her down twice more before I explode and thank God I'm wearing a condom, because that performance would've gotten her pregnant for sure.

I collapse against the cushions, and she collapses on my chest. Her lips touch my neck ever so gently, and it makes my dick twitch inside her.

"Thank you," she whispers so quietly I can't be sure she actually said anything.

"For what?" I ask. My lips are pressed to her forehead.

She pushes up on me until she's looking me in the eye. "For listening and letting me cry on you. For taking my mind off everything." She looks down at her dress and then back up at me. "I'm going to go change. Are you sticking around?"

Carrington doesn't wait for my answer. She just lifts up, whimpering a little when my softening cock slides out of her.

Her steps are slow as she disappears into her bedroom. I should take this as my chance to get out of here, but I can't make myself get up and leave. She still seems a little emotional, which I can't blame her. Thank God she showed up at her cousin's fiancé's place when she did, but then again she could've gotten really hurt too. Tomorrow I'll see what I can find out and make sure that the man who attacked Abby stays behind bars.

A few minutes later, she comes out in knit shorts and a t-shirt. Her long hair is twisted up on top of her head. She looks young and fresh-faced with no makeup on, but no less beautiful.

"Are you hungry?" she asks me as she walks through the living room and into the kitchen.

"I'm okay, but I'd take something to drink if you got it."

I sit at the breakfast bar and watch her move around her tiny kitchen. She opens the refrigerator, bends at the waist, and pulls out a bottle of beer. Carrington moves around the counter and stops between my legs. She holds my attention as she tips the bottle back, taking a healthy swallow.

She pulls it away from her mouth, wraps an arm around my neck, and kisses me. I've never met someone as forward as she is, but I like it. I grab her around the waist and pull her toward me so she's flush against me. It's a short kiss, but still it's enough to turn me on again. She pulls back and hands me the beer. Carrington is unlike any girl or woman I've ever met.

Chapter Seven

Carrington

I pull into the driveway of my parents' home and climb out of my car. It's been three days since Abby was attacked. Ben's been so great for my cousin. He hasn't left her side since it happened. Natalie has been attached to Abby too. That poor little girl was there when it happened. I know Abby prevented Natalie from seeing much.

I took them some ice cream earlier and almost cried when I saw Abby's face. It was still swollen, and her nose was very clearly broken. It was double its normal size. She still had a really bad headache, but the ER doctor said that it should lessen as the swelling went down.

When I step inside, I find my dad and brother sitting in the living room, watching baseball.

"Hey, guys."

I bend down, kiss my dad's cheek, and ruffle my brother's hair. "Quit it," he growls before trying to grab for me, but I dodge him and laugh as I make my way toward the kitchen. I find my mom standing in front of the stove, dressed in yoga pants and a form-fitting t-shirt. At forty-six, my mom is in the best shape. Between her dancing and her personal training, she's lean and cut.

"Hey, Mom." She wraps me in her arms. I return the hug and let her hold me tight.

"I saw Abby today," I whisper.

"I went with your aunt Journey this morning to take Journey and Abby to breakfast. It took all I had not to cry when I saw her face. Journey's upset because she feels like Abby doesn't need her now that Abby's got Ben looking after her. It's not true, but Journey's still really upset and emotional and understandably so. Ben is taking very good care of Abby, so she's got nothing to worry about." She pulls back and tucks my hair behind my ears. "You're being safe, aren't you? You know, keeping the deadbolt locked, leaving lights on?"

I've missed this closeness that my mom and I used to have, back before it became clear that I was always going to be competing with the memory of a ghost. My eyes burn, but I hold the tears back. "I'm careful, I promise."

After that little emotional exchange, I help her finish making dinner and then set the table. We all sit around the table and listen to my brother talk about school and his excitement about going to training camp this summer. Normally it'd bother me that they're all focused on Luke and how great he is, but for once I'm glad because I hate lying to them when they ask me about work.

My phone vibrates in my pocket, and I pull it out

and glance at it. It's a text from Damien.

I want to see you.

Since that's all it says, I decide to stick it back in my pocket for now. No one notices. I get goose bumps just thinking about that man. He is so good looking, but not in the classical sense. He's covered in tattoos up to his neck; he has those gauges in his ears. I've always been drawn to the typical bad boys, but Damien is so much more than just a bad boy. He's dangerous, and I should keep my distance, but I can't, at least not yet.

The thought of seeing him again does something to me. I've never seen a more beautiful cock in my entire life. Sure, I'm only twenty-one, but I've seen enough in-person or in movies to know that his is beautiful. It's long, thick with the right amount of girth. Oh shit, my nipples are getting hard just thinking about it.

Sunday night, he slept over and that was all we did. After the rendezvous on the sofa, we watched TV for a little bit and then he came to bed with me. I'd never really been a fan of having a guy sleep with me, but when he pulled me against him, I nuzzled in close.

When I woke up, he was gone, but again he left a note.

"Care bear?" I look up from my plate, and my dad is staring at me expectantly.

"I'm sorry, what?"

"I just asked how work at the hospital's going and if you've seen anything exciting." My dad gives me a bright smile that makes my heart ache a little since again I have to lie.

"Oh, it's going good. We see all sorts of stuff at night. Alcohol poisoning, fights and accidents are what we see for the most part. I've learned a lot since I've been there."

My mom smiles at me. "That's so great. We're so proud of you and the work you're doing."

"Thanks." After that, I shift the focus back to my brother. "So, Wukey, what are you going to do for your birthday?" He turns eighteen in a few weeks.

"Stop calling me Wukey, dork. I don't know what I'm going to do yet. Are you going to buy me a present?" He gives me the same smile I'm sure he gives all those teenybopper girls to charm them, but I'm immune to my brother's charms.

"Maybe, if I feel like it." I reach over and pinch his arm.

"Ow, bitch," he yelps. Then he pinches me. I slap at his arm until our dad stops us.

"All right, you two, stop. Luke, watch your language."

I stick my tongue out at my brother, and he flips me off. After we finish eating, my brother and I clear the table and load the dishwasher. We work side by side, and I ask, "So, how's school? Still getting straight A's?"

"It's good, easy, a piece of cake." Of course it is. Again, my brother excels at everything.

Not only is my brother extremely athletic, but he's also super smart. He's graduating a semester early because he's already met all of his requirements.

I know I sound jealous, and maybe I am, but I've had to work my ass off for every A or B I've ever gotten whereas Luke barely studies and he aces everything.

After we finish up, he grabs me and pulls me into a hug. He's three years younger than me but towers over me. "Are you okay?"

"Yeah, why?" I ask, pulling back to look up into his face that looks identical to our dad's.

"Well, you know, with everything that happened to Abby. That's the second time you've shown up after that asshole attacked her. I'm just glad they've finally caught that piece of shit," Luke says.

"I'm good. Just glad, like you, but also glad that she's got someone like Ben who'll make sure she's taken care of." I couldn't have picked a better person for Abby to fall in love with.

"Joe and Parker really like their sister's guy, and Ben's little girl is adorable," Luke says.

I give him a hug and tell him I'll invite him over one night to celebrate his birthday.

I hug and kiss my dad goodbye, and when I go to say bye to my mom she tells me that she's walking me out. Her arm is looped through mine as we make our way down the walkway toward my car.

"Honey, I was thinking that maybe one day next week, you and I could do a spa day. What do you think?"

"That'd be great. Whenever you want." I'm excited that she wants to do a mom and daughter day.

I climb into my car and wave to her before backing out of the driveway. When I hit the end of the street, I pull over, pull out my cellphone, and text Damien back.

Your place or mine?

I sit in my car and wait for him to answer me, which happens a few minutes later.

He tells me to come to his place and texts me his address. I look at myself in the rearview mirror and make sure that I look fine. My hair is in a braid that rests over my shoulder, and I'm wearing a pink zipped-up hoodie over a white tank top and black short shorts. I should run home and change, but I'm not too worried about it because I'm sure Damien couldn't care less about what I'm wearing.

Damien lives just outside of Saint Helena Island. I pull into the parking lot of his complex and park in visitor parking. The lawn is green and lush, there aren't a lot of trees, but colorful flowers make up a lot of the landscaping. He appears on the walkway and gives me a smile that makes me weak in the knees.

I run toward him and jump into his arms, wrapping my legs around his waist. "Hi," I say lamely. I feel him begin to move as we make our way to his apartment.

"What did you do today?" he asks before placing his lips on my neck.

"Went to see Abby today and then had dinner at my parents' house."

He opens a door, and we step inside his apartment. He sets me down, and I look around.

"How's your cousin doing?" I turn to look up at

him.

"She's okay. Her face is so swollen still, but Ben's taking good care of her."

I look around his apartment, and all I can say is that it's decorated total bachelor style. The living room has a fireplace with a flat screen adorning the wall above it. He has an overstuffed loveseat against the wall with a worn-looking coffee table and two matching end tables next to it. I see an Xbox on the floor by the fireplace and a stack of games.

Damien wraps his arms around my waist, pulling me back until I'm flush against him.

"That's good that she's got someone watching her back. You said he's with the sheriff's department, right?"

"Yeah, so I think that gives all of us peace of mind. Show me the rest of your place?" I turn in his arms and look up into his eyes. I can't decide if they're hazel or green.

He leads me into a bright kitchen that's pretty bare but surprisingly clean. We move down the hall, and he shows me the bathroom, which has a big counter with double sinks. The shower is a stand up with all glass and duel showerheads. The tub is so deep that you'd feel like you were sinking into it.

We go to the door at the end of the hall, and I know it's his bedroom. A huge bed against the wall dominates the space. There's a nightstand and lamp next to it and then a dresser on the other side of the room. I like all of the natural light that comes in from the large windows. The room smells like him, fresh and woodsy.

"Do you want a drink? I think all I have is beer and water." He grabs my hand to pull me out of his room.

"I'll take a beer." I follow him into the kitchen, and he pulls a couple of bottles out. He opens and hands me one. "Thanks." I let the cold beer slide down my throat.

"Have you been studying for your boards?"

I hadn't planned on telling Damien about not passing my test and why I started working at The Thirsty Beaver, but while we were lying in my bed it just sort of came out.

"Yeah, I studied all day yesterday. The test is a little over a month away, and I'm already freaking out. I can take it as many times as I need to, but I don't know if I can keep putting myself through the stress again and again." I take another swig of my beer.

"You said that your grades were good in school. It was just your boards that you didn't pass, right?"

"Right. I don't know, it's just…I know all of the information, but my mind goes blank." It's testing anxiety, I know it, but I don't know how to get past it.

He comes around to me. "Let me help you. Give me some time to think about it, but I would love to see you out of The Beaver."

"Okay, sure. Thanks." I know he hates me dancing. He's never come right out and said it, but I know he does.

We go outside to the deck, and instead of sitting in my own chair Damien pulls me down onto his lap. "We need to keep this just between us when we're at the club."

"I figured as much. I know you hate me dancing, but are you going to be able to handle it when I'm on stage?" I turn sideways in his lap and look at him. His jaw is clenched.

Reaching up, I stroke his chin with my fingers while I wait for him to answer. "I can handle it. I'm just not going to like it."

"Well, just pretend that we're the only two people in the club and that I'm dancing for you. Hell, most of the time I'm imagining I'm dancing for you any way."

I lean in and kiss his lips. The kiss is slow, and it makes me all tingly. When I pull back, he reaches out and strokes my bottom lip with his thumb.

We finish our beers and then head inside to watch a movie. In the dark, with the movie playing, my eyes begin to feel heavy. I rest my head in his lap, and Damien strokes my hair until I fall asleep.

Chapter Eight

Damien

My eyes open, and I find Carrington gone. I slide my hand over her spot and find it still warm. I roll onto my back and stare up at the ceiling. Last night Carrington fell asleep with her head in my lap while we watched a movie. When it was over, I was going to wake her so she could go home. Letting her stay was entering dangerous ground, but I loved the way she snuggled into me. I carried her into my room and then laid her down on my bed, climbing in behind her. She fit against me perfectly, and I loved that she snuggled in as close as humanly possible.

The sound of music coming from the living room brings me out of my thoughts. I throw my boxer briefs on and make my way down the hall. What I see stops me in my tracks. Carrington is standing in the middle of my living room in her bra and panties with her hair piled up on her head.

The tempo of the music picks up, and then she starts to move. I know nothing about dance, but the

69

way she moves and twirls around my living room has me in awe. Obviously, I knew she could dance, but this is so much more. Her muscles contract as she moves. She kicks her leg up, grabs it, and spins around. She does complex-looking kicks that have her completely in the air.

My dick is hard as hell as I watch her move. When she finishes, I move toward her, wrapping my arms around her waist. "That was beautiful, baby." I run my tongue up the side of her neck, tasting the saltiness of her skin.

"Thank you. Contemporary dance is kind of my thing. I love letting the music flow through me and guide me. The music didn't wake you, did it?" She turns in my arms and wraps her arms around my waist.

"No, it didn't. You better put a shirt on or something before I take you right here." I reach around and slap her ass. "Put one of my t-shirts on."

She wiggles her tight ass at me as she moves down the hall to my bedroom. Shaking my head, I head to the kitchen to start breakfast.

Carrington joins me a few minutes later in one of my black button-up shirts with the sleeves rolled up. She's drowning in it, but damn if she doesn't look sexy as fuck. "So what do you have planned tonight?" I ask her.

"I actually picked up a shift in the ER tonight. Are you working at the club?"

"Yeah, I have to take care of business for the club. So what do you do in the ER?" I hope it's nothing that puts her at risk for getting hurt. I can't afford to worry about her all night long.

"I'm pretty much a slave to the nurses. I get the patients stuff, clean up rooms after they leave, help transport to the floors if they get admitted, and sometimes play babysitter to kids when we're treating the parents. It's not glamorous, but it's where I want to work once I pass my boards, or I should say if I pass them." I hate seeing the embarrassed look on her face.

"Hey, you'll pass it. I'm gonna help, remember." I tuck a strand of hair behind her ear, and I lean forward, pressing my lips to hers.

My phone rings, and I grab it off of the counter. "It's Rafe. Can you watch the bacon? I need to take this call."

She hops off the counter, and I walk to my bedroom and shut the door. "Hey, Rafe. What's up?"

"Damien, my man. I've got some shit I need you to do. You know what we talked about Saturday night? Well, we're ready to move forward. We've got some grade A pussy coming to the club, and a few of the dancers want in. Friday night we've got a bachelor party coming in, and they've rented out the room. They want at least three girls and some blow. I need you to talk to Cari."

"Okay, but why do I need to talk to her?" *Please don't say she's got to do it*, I repeat over and over to myself.

"They've personally requested her. If not to fuck, they at least want some lap dances. She'll get a cut of the room. If she just does the lap dances, we can even have security in there to make sure they don't try anything. What do you think?"

Rage fills me, and I seriously want to reach through the phone and rip his fucking face off. I clench my fist in my lap so tight that my knuckles are white.

"I doubt she'll be down for fucking, but she'll do the lap dances. I do want to be the one in there, though. I have faith in my men, but it's easy to get swayed by the mighty dollar and she's our biggest moneymaker. I don't want to lose her because some douche crossed the line and one of our men let it happen. What about the coke?"

"Tonight I'll give you the money to go get it. The person I work for has made arrangements for the exchange."

Rafe tells me that he'll give me the address when I come in tonight. Carrington has to pass that test. I won't make it through this assignment if something happens to her. Why couldn't she have been a mediocre waitress without any interest in dancing?

I end the call and take a deep breath. This is where things are going to start getting crazy. Right now I'm purely gathering Intel, getting myself accepted into the inner circle and reporting back to my superiors.

The smell of bacon pulls me out of my thoughts, and I follow the scent. Rounding the corner, I find Carrington moving around my kitchen. It's domestic and a complete turn on, especially since she's wearing just my shirt.

"Sit down and I'll bring your plate to you," she says, not even looking at me. A minute later and she carries two plates to the table. She gives me a kiss as she hands me mine. Carrington sits down across from me, and we dig in.

We sit in a companionable silence. These eggs are the best I've ever had, and I moan with each fork full. She smiles at me and then takes a big bite of her bacon.

"Was there a problem at the club?"

"No, he just wanted to let me know we've got a big party coming in tomorrow night."

It's a lame as hell excuse, but I can't tell her anything else, and I don't know how to tell her that the party requested she be the main entertainment. She may still have to dance privately for them, and I don't want her feeling awkward.

She watches me from across the table, and I wonder if she even believes the shit I'm saying. "Oh, okay." She picks her plate up and grabs mine for me. I hear her scrape the plates off and then rinse them off.

"You don't have to clean up," I tell her, walking into the kitchen to make coffee. "Can you stay for a little bit? Maybe sit outside and drink coffee?"

"Yeah, sure." Her mouth spreads into such a wide smile that I can't help but return it. This girl is something else.

***

It's six o'clock when I step into the club. Sundays through Thursdays, the club is pretty quiet. The dancers are okay but nowhere near the caliber of the girls who dance on Friday and Saturday. We have two bartenders working and no waitresses. I give one of the bartenders, Kyle, a chin lift and make my way back toward Rafe and Tucker's office.

A quick knock on the door and I pop it open. I find Rafe sitting behind his desk and Tucker standing next to him. They're both looking at the computer screen. Neither of them looks up, but they signal for me to come in with their hands. I sit down in front of their desk and wait for them to talk to me.

Rafe looks up at me and gives me a chin lift. He sets a thick envelope on the desk in front of me. I pick it up and peer inside. It's a large stack of hundred dollar bills. He reaches out to me with a piece of paper.

"Here's the address. You'll be hooking up with a guy named Tony. He'll take the cash and then he'll have a small duffle bag for you." I pick up the address. "Damien, we're trusting you with this. Don't let us down."

"Don't worry, you can trust me. I'll be back ASAP. Do they know to expect me, not you?"

"Yeah, they know our head of security is coming. Take this with you just in case."

Tucker opens a drawer and pulls out a .22. I take it from him, check the clip, and tuck it into the back of my jeans, pulling my t-shirt out so it covers the gun. I take the money and take my leave. Out in the parking lot, I stick the money in the glove box of my Jeep. I punch in the address on my GPS.

It's a twenty-minute drive, giving me lots of time to think about things, about Carrington. I shouldn't be fucking her because if I were to get compromised, it could be bad for her. I'm a selfish bastard though, and I don't care since I'm not done fucking her out of my system yet. In all seriousness, I want to help her pass her boards so she can stop fucking dancing. As much as I love watching her and fantasize about her dancing just for me, she deserves so much better than that life.

I pull down a street filled with McMansions. Each house is big and looks identical to the next. The GPS tells me I've reached my destination when I pull up in front of the monstrosity at the end of the street. If their plan was to look inconspicuous, then they've failed. The house itself looks normal, but the landscaping is ridiculous. The shrubbery is shaped like animals, and there are so many flowers gracing the yard that I can't even tell if there's grass.

There is also the large man wearing his sunglasses at night, standing by the front door. I get out of my jeep and make my way toward the front door. The guy with the sunglasses is watching me as I make my approach.

"Can I help you?" His voice is deep.

"Yeah, Rafe sent me." I'm not scared, but this guy does make me uneasy. I'm not a small man, and this man is huge compared to me.

"Turn around. I need to pat you down." *Well, shit.*

"Just to let you know, I have a .22 in the back of my jeans." He grabs it from me, stuffs it in his pants, and finishes frisking me.

"You can have it back when you leave. Go on in, have a seat in the first room on the right. Someone will be with you shortly."

Opening the door, I step inside and notice the inside is just as gaudy as the outside. Gold is everywhere. It's like they're trying too hard to prove something. I commit everything I see to memory and step inside the room I was instructed to have a seat in. The artwork that fills the room is erotic; there are sculptures of people in various sexual positions and photographs of naked women in various poses.

Carrington immediately comes to mind. What I wouldn't give to have some photos of her like that. I quickly banish those thoughts because I don't need to get an erection right now. Before I can push the thoughts away, two women step into the room and sit on both sides of me. The one on my left puts her hand on my thigh.

"Hey, big boy. Are you looking for some company? You look like the kind of guy who could handle both of us." I turn and look at the girl who said it and can tell right away she's high as a kite. Her pupils are dilated, and she's got a tiny bit of white powder in her nostril.

"I'm sure I could, but I'm not interested. I'm just here to pick something up." As if right on cue, a man a little shorter than me enters the room. He's carrying a small duffle bag.

Both girls immediately get up and go to him. I control my features when he grabs the chin of the one who propositioned me and turns her face toward him.

"Were you in my stash again? If you're going to touch my shit, the least you could do is clean your fucking nose off before you come out to speak to any potential clients." With the quickness of a snake striking its prey, the mystery man backhands the girl. "Go get cleaned up before I get rid of you."

He watches the two girls scramble away and then turns back to me. I can tell he's sizing me up the way his eyes travel up and down my body. It's certainly not in a sexual manner, but more curiosity. He's probably wondering if he can best me if need be.

"You Rafe's boy?"

"I'm no one's boy, but yeah, I work for Rafe. Is that the package?" I motion with my head toward the bag in his hand.

"You got the cash?"

I hand him the envelope and watch as he opens it and counts it. He hands me the bag. I unzip it and look inside. There are two large bricks of coke inside. "Looks good."

"You work at their club, right?" I nod my head. "That dancer they've got...Pepper, is it? I'd like a piece of her. Maybe we could work something out. Tell Rafe I'll be in touch."

Schooling my features, I nod my head and head toward the front door. Big man at the door hands me back my gun, so I tuck it back in my pants and make my way toward my Jeep. My blood pressure is rising, and I'm ready to go ballistic. I'll be damned if I let that drug dealing, pimping piece of shit anywhere near Carrington. She has to pass that test. If I could afford it, I'd pay for her to survive until she could take and pass that goddamn test.

As I drive back to the bar, I know I've got someone following me. Too bad whoever it is sucks at it. I clocked him tailing me about five minutes after I left. He fucked up my plan to call my handler. I can't risk it. The guy could have equipment on him to listen to any calls that I'd make. All I want to do is get rid of the blow and go bury myself in Carrington's sweet pussy.

That thought right there is why I should stay away from her, but I'm a selfish prick.

I'm finally back at The Thirsty Beaver and pull into the parking lot. My tail cruises right on by, thank fuck. I grab the bag and head back inside.

Chapter Nine

Carrington

I stick my pencil behind my ear as I read through my notes. I'm taking my retest in a month because I want to give myself ample time to study. There is no way in hell that I'm going to fail this test this time. I can't. I grab the study guide that I paid almost $200 for and the sticky tabs I bought so I can hopefully resell the guides when I'm done. My phone beeps, and I pick it up to find a text from Abby.

Hey girl, can we have lunch someday soon? I miss you.

I smile at my phone.

Absolutely! How about you and Natalie meet me Tuesday?

Since Abby's attack, she's been very protective

of Natalie, like never letting her out of her sight protective.

Sounds great, maybe we can pick up lunch and bring it to you.

Abby's embarrassed about her nose, which is still swollen, and there is still some bruising under her eyes. Plus, she sounds very nasally when she talks. The bastard who raped her is set to go to trial soon. I'm surprised by how swiftly everything is happening, but I'm glad. I just want Abby to get the closure that will help her move on.

After agreeing with her, I place my phone back on the table and pick up my study guide, beginning to study about how to assess someone with mid-sternal chest pain.

My latte is cold now since I've lost two hours while in the study zone. I tip it back and drink it down anyway because I still need to study for at least another hour and I'm freaking exhausted. I need to come up with a proper schedule so that I don't study and work myself into exhaustion because then my parents might find out that I'm stripping. I'm afraid what my dad would do or what they would think of me. Since high school, I've been their problem child, especially when I discovered boys and began dressing a little provocatively: short shorts, short skirts, tight shirts and tight jeans. I used to skip school, and a few times I got busted drinking and making out with boys.

I hated high school. The boys all wanted me, and

the girls hated me and loved calling me a slut and a whore. The worst was when my English teacher my junior year came on to me, promising me an A if he could "play" with me. I was so freaked out I didn't go to school for three days. My dad and mom finally had an intervention as to why I wasn't going to school and hiding in my room.

When I told them what the pervert said to me, my dad was beyond livid. He hopped right in his truck and took off. My mom and I had jumped in her car and went up to the high school. As soon as we walked into the office, we could already hear my dad yelling at the principal, demanding that Mr. Travis be fired immediately.

At the end of it all, Mr. Travis resigned and moved away. For a long time, my dad acted like he couldn't even look at me, and the kids at school loved the pervy teacher so they all blamed me for what happened. It had been such a dark time for me. I started acting out—smoking weed and drinking until my dad and I hashed things out. I still feel like I've been nothing but a huge disappointment to them. The dancing is just another thing for me to do to make him disappointed.

I was really trying to do better, to be better. I graduated from nursing school with a B-plus average and felt confident when I took my boards, but then I found out I didn't pass.

I walk to the little coffee shop inside the library and order another latte, trying to keep any negative thoughts from my mind. Once my hot beverage is in my hand, I head back to my study area. My phone beeps at me, and I pick it up to find a text from

Damien.

What are you doing?

I've been studying for the past three hours. U?

He answers me almost immediately.

Nothing. I just got up. Feel like taking a break? I could come get you.

A warm tingling sensation fills my belly when I read his words. He wants to spend time with me. I should really tell him no so I can study, but honestly I could use a break.

Yeah okay. I'll have to warn you I'm looking a little scary. My hair is piled up on my head, I've got no makeup on, and I'm in a t-shirt and jogging shorts.

I tell him what library I'm at, and he tells me he'll be here in ten minutes to get me. I shove my study guides back into my messenger back and scoop up my latte as I head toward the front door.

Sure enough, ten minutes goes by and then I see Damien's blue Jeep pull into the parking lot. I walk swiftly to the Jeep and climb inside. He surprises me by reaching across and grabbing me, pulling me to him. A gasp leaves my lips right before they come in contact with his. It's a slow kiss. He knows how to invoke an ache deep in my belly, and all too soon it's over. Bummer.

Damien stares at my lips and then grunts something unintelligibly. He puts the Jeep into drive and pulls out onto the main road. We pull into Subway, grab a couple of sandwiches, and head toward the beach. We get out of the car, and he lifts me so I'm sitting on the hood. I watch him climb up and sit next to me.

"So what made you decide to be a nurse?" Damien asks before taking a bite of his sandwich.

"I don't know. I guess I've always just wanted to be one. My mom says I used to bandage up my dolls and teddy bears. She even said I wrapped a whole roll of toilet paper around my younger brother's head and then told everyone I had to take his brain out," I say with a laugh. "I love it; that's why I have to pass my boards. Sure, I love dancing in any form, but nursing is what I need to do."

He cups my neck in his hand and pulls me toward him. He looks deeply into my eyes. "You're going to pass, I know it."

"What if I don't? My parents already think I'm a failure." Ugh, my stupid eyes fill with tears. I'm not a crier, dammit.

"Baby, I'm sure that's not true." He places his lips against my forehead.

I spill my guts to him. I tell him about everything. When I get to the part about my old teacher, Damien's fingers spasm against my neck. I don't like the look that crosses his face, but just as quickly it disappears.

"I had an older sister. She died while my mom was still pregnant with her." I don't know why I'm telling him this. "Sometimes I feel like I'm competing with her ghost. You don't know what it's like to watch your parents mourn a child that's been gone for such a long time and feeling like second best." I drag my hands down my face. "Sorry. What about you? Are you an only child?"

"Yeah, it's just me. Don't apologize for how you feel. Have you told them that you feel that way?" I shake my head. "Babe, you should. They probably have no idea that they've made you feel this way."

"I'll think about it."

We finish our sandwiches, and I rest my head on his shoulder as we both silently watch the surf. Music from his radio creates the backdrop for us. The sun is beating down on my skin, but there is a cool breeze coming off of the water. Damien wraps his arm around my shoulders when I begin to get goosebumps.

A part of me wants to ask Damien what it is that we're doing, but I don't dare. I'm starting to care about him, and if he doesn't feel the same way, I would be humiliated. I hear a song I love on the radio. I hop down and turn it up and begin dancing around in the sand in front of his Jeep. I smile up at him as I bring my arms above my head and swivel my hips.

He shakes his head at me as a smile graces his sexy, full lips. When the song ends I move toward him, but he hops down as another song, a slower song, begins. He lifts me up until my legs are wrapped around his waist and my arms wrapped around his neck. Damien surprises me as he begins to sway side to side to the music. He's just full of surprises, and he's making it harder and harder to resist him.

"Thank you for the break," I whisper before kissing his lips. It's a sweet, gentle glide that ends far too quickly. He carries me toward the Jeep with me still wrapped around him. I hear him open the door and then feel my butt hit the seat. I pull him toward me one more time. He grinds his hard dick against the apex of my thighs. Damien licks the seam of my lips, and I open to him.

I could kiss him all day, but unfortunately he pulls away. "I should get you back. Do you need to sleep before work tonight?"

"I probably should. Again, thank you for this," I tell him. He gives me a smile that makes me tingle before shutting my door and walking around to his.

As we head back toward the library, I'm taken aback when he reaches for my hand and intertwines his fingers with mine, holding my hand until we reach the parking lot of the library. He parks his Jeep right next to my car.

"I'll see you tonight," I tell him as I grab my bag out of the backseat.

"Yeah. Remember, babe, they can't know about us. It's not a rule or anything, but I'm worried it could mean problems for us."

A part of me feels like he just might be embarrassed that he's sleeping with a stripper, even though he works at a gentleman's club. I paste on my huge fake smile.

"I won't say anything. I'll pretend you don't exist."

I smile at him before shutting the door and climbing into my car. Why do I care that he wants

to keep me a secret? I pull out of my spot and give him a wave before pulling away.

On my way home, I think about everything that I talked about with Damien today. I've never been good at sharing stuff, but with him I let it all out. I guess maybe it's because I was thinking about it earlier. Who the hell knows?

***

I add another coat of mascara to my lashes and then use the eyelash curler to get them just right. My lips are painted candy apple red. On my way home from the library earlier, I decided to go look at a store in Charleston that sells risqué costumes all year round. It took me about two minutes to find the costume I wanted.

Since I've started dancing here, I've tried making friends with some of the other dancers, but they've all done nothing but treat me like I'm diseased or something. I know they think I slept with one of the bosses to get the headlining dancer position, which of course I didn't, but they wouldn't listen to me when I promised them that I didn't.

Taylor has been my only friend since I started, and I'm very thankful for that.

I slip my costume on and stand up in front of the mirror, adjusting it until it looks just right. My black thigh high boots compliment my entire get up, and I can't wait to see what Damien thinks of it. Of course he won't say anything, because every time I've seen him tonight he's ignored me. I wasn't expecting it to hurt as much as it did.

Taylor sticks her head in, takes one look at me, and squeals. "You look hot." She taps the bill of my hat. "They're going to freak."

"Thanks." I slap her on the ass and make my way backstage.

"All right, boys. Pepper has got a special treat for you tonight."

I hear the whistles and the catcalls and take a deep breath. It certainly doesn't get any easier. Butterflies still flutter around in my stomach those few minutes before I go on.

The beginning notes of "Dude (Looks Like a Lady)" come on, and I begin to move. I hate to toot my own horn, but I'm on fire tonight. My hips shake as I move toward the first pole, wrapping my hands around it and gripping it with my knees as I spin around it. I stop with my back to the crowd and arch my back as I roll my hips. Facing the crowd, I squat down while I grab my breasts over my dress and stick out my tongue, pretending that I'm going to lick them.

With a few more twirls, I remove my cop's uniform and crawl across the floor. The song finally ends. The crowd goes crazy, and when I go to step off of the stage, I feel arms band around my waist and I go flying off of the stage until I'm in some asshole's lap. He gropes my boob as I struggle to get away from him.

"Where you going, baby?" he slurs.

"Let me go," I shout, right before I cock my fist back and punch him right in the face. He squeezes me tight, but then I'm up in the air.

"You okay?" Damien whispers in my ear. I sag

against his chest.

"I hurt my hand," I tell him as I watch Rafe and one of the other bouncers grab the guy and drag him through the club. His jaw clenches as he picks up my injured hand. It's swelling up already. Damien carries me back to Bridgette's office since she's not in tonight. He sets me on top of her desk.

"Fuck! I should kick his ass for touching you." He cups my face in his hands and leans down, kissing my lips. "I'm sorry I've ignored you tonight. Is there any chance I could get you to wear that costume one night?"

Damien's lip quirks up in the corner, and he tells me to sit tight while he gets me some ice. At least he made me smile.

"Girl, are you okay?" Taylor comes running toward me. "I saw what happened. That guy grabbed you so fast it took everyone by surprise, but man you sure clocked him good."

"Thanks, but now I think my hand is messed up." Taylor looks down at it and winces.

I'm probably going to need to go to the emergency room to have it x-rayed, but I'll wait until Damien gets back and tell him. She tells me she'll call me tomorrow and disappears out of the room when Damien comes back.

"How's it feel, baby?" He says "baby" in almost a whisper. It does bad things to my insides when he calls me that, and by bad, I mean very good.

"I should probably have it looked at. If it's not broken, then it's probably sprained. What'll happen if I can't dance?"

I worry my bottom lip with my teeth. I was

supposed to do some sort of special lap dance for someone in one of the private rooms tonight. He supposedly asked for me. Will I be fired?

"Nothing's going to happen to you, I promise. I'm going to have Taylor help you get changed back into your street clothes, and I'm going to take you to have it looked at." He looks toward the door, which is still closed, and turns back toward me. Damien's lips touch mine before he pulls away. "Come on."

He helps me off of the desk and leads me out into the hall. Behind Rafe's door, I can hear flesh hitting flesh, grunts and groans. I look up at Damien with wide eyes and let him lead me away. The guy was just some drunk asshole. I didn't want him getting hurt. I just wanted him to let go of me. We stop at the bar, where Taylor is standing.

Damien instructs her to help me change and to bring me out front when I'm done. Taylor is such a dork. She gives Damien a salute before leading me to the dressing room.

***

"Do you need anything else, baby?" Damien tucks me into my bed and kisses me. We just got back from both the ER and the all-night pharmacy. My hand isn't broken, but I did sprain my wrist. Now I have to wear a splint and can't dance for at least two weeks. I'll have to go to my doctor to follow up next week. The pain pills they prescribed are starting to kick in, and now I'm feeling a little woozy.

"No, I'm good. Thank you for taking care of me. Are they going to be mad that I can't dance?"

He strips down to his boxer-briefs and climbs in on the other side. Damien pulls me into his arms before answering. "No, babe. They completely understood when I called Rafe to tell him. They're just worried about you and feel bad that the douche bag even laid his hands on you at all. Get some sleep, yeah?"

I snuggle up to him so my back is against his front and feel my eyes drift shut.

Chapter Ten

Damien

My footsteps echo on the tile floor as I walk back toward Rafe's office. He called me an hour ago and requested my presence. I really wanted to tell him to fuck off because Carrington was kissing a trail down my stomach, toward my dick, but I wasn't sure if he wanted to talk about the guy from last night. I knock and wait until I hear someone tell me to come in.

I close the door behind me and take a seat in the chair across from Rafe. Tucker sits in the chair next to me. "What's up, guys?"

"How's Carrington?" Rafe asks.

"She's okay. The pain pills have knocked her out, so she's not up for long after she takes one. She is worried about losing her job since she can't dance or waitress."

Rafe leans forward. "Tell our girl that she's got nothing to worry about. Also tell her that the piece of shit is banned from here."

"Not like he'll be doing much moving yet," Tucker says with a snicker.

"Did you guys fuck him up good? It sounded like it."

"Fuck yes we did. He touched our star. We lost at least a grand since she didn't get a chance to work the back room and do those lap dances we promised those customers. I'll call her later and let her know that she doesn't need to worry about money while she can't work. We'll make sure she's taken care of."

It's taking all of my strength to keep my face impassive. I'll be damned if they make sure she's taken care of. She's fucking mine. *Fuck*, I think to myself. That thought needs to go. She's not mine; she can't be.

"Great. I'm sure she'll appreciate that. I know she was worried about losing her job." I get up to leave, but Tucker stops me.

"We just wanted you to know we have another run for you to do. We made two thousand dollars in profit the other night. We're already booked until December."

"That's great! That's what you guys wanted. You know me—I'm here to help with whatever."

I need to find out who's pulling Rafe and Tucker's strings. The guy I bought the blow from didn't give us anything useful, so I'm going to keep working the brothers.

I head out to my Jeep and then make my way toward Carrington's apartment. She was asleep when I left, so I grabbed her keys. When I went to leave earlier, I peeked in on her. She was hugging her wrist to her chest, pissing me off even more.

With a box of donuts I picked up, I make my way toward her apartment. I unlock the door and am greeted by silence. I set the donuts on her kitchen counter and start a pot of coffee. While it brews, I head back to Carrington's bedroom and find that she's knocked out and snoring. I head back to the kitchen and grab an ice pack out of the freezer and again head back into her room. This time she's sitting up, looking disoriented and in pain. She looks at me, and I feel something shift inside of me. Warmth spreads across my chest, and my heart beats rapidly in my chest. It feels like the bottom drops out of my stomach. Her hair is in a haphazard ponytail that's moved to the side, her face is free of makeup, and there's a dried drool trail on her chin.

"What time is it?" Her voice is sluggish. I walk toward her, reaching out and tucking her hair behind her ear.

"It's eleven. How's the wrist?"

I sit down next to her and carefully take her wrist in my hand, holding the ice pack on it. She winces a little, but they said they pain should lessen in forty-eight to seventy-two hours. It's too soon to take a pain pill so she's going to have to suffer for a bit longer.

"It's sore, but I'll live. They're not firing me, are they?"

"No, baby, they're not. They'll make sure you have money. They don't want you to worry about anything. I'm going to go, but there are donuts on the counter and I made you coffee. Wait until after you eat before you take another pain pill." I stand up and feel her hand on my arm.

"You're leaving?"

"Sorry, I've got shit to do. I'll check in with you later." Bending down, I kiss her lips before leaving.

As soon as the door to her apartment closes behind me, I take a deep breath. She's working her way under my skin, and it's not a good thing. I'm great at reading people, and I can tell that she has feelings for me. I have to pull back—I have to. Everything she knows about me is a lie, and that's not fair to her. How could we really work? When she finds out I lied about who I am, she'd break up with me anyway.

Plus, at any time, my case could go south and I don't want her caught in the middle. I'd never forgive myself. I can't help but feel pissed off as I move toward my truck. Not being ready to end things but knowing I need to fucking sucks. The best way to do that is just to begin treating her like shit again.

***

It's been a week since Carrington got hurt, and I haven't spoken to her since. She texted me and called me the first couple of days, but I didn't respond. I know when she sent her final text because she didn't hold back.

I don't know what your problem is, but if you're done with me at least have the balls to tell me. You don't need to though, because I'm done with you, you asshole!

At least I'll get another week before I have to see her again. I thought about going out and banging as many women as I could so I could forget about her, but I couldn't do it. It's not like my dick's broken, but none of them hold a candle to her. She's who I want, but I can't fucking have her. Now it's got me in a perpetually bad mood.

I step inside the club and freeze. Carrington is standing at the bar in a tiny skirt and a top tied up under her breasts. The brace on her wrist still gets my blood boiling, but it's no longer my job to worry. Well, that's at least what I tell myself.

Schooling my features, I stomp over to her. "What the fuck are you doing here? Didn't they tell you to take at least two weeks off?"

She looks up at me, and there is a fire in her eyes. "Not that it's any of your business, but my doctor cleared me to come back to work. Rafe says I can wait tables for a week and then go back to dancing. If you don't like it…Fuck…Off."

She grabs her tray and heads back toward the rooms for the private parties. My blood starts to boil. I don't want her back there.

I make my way back to Rafe's office and walk right in. He's in his office, alone. "We need to talk."

Rafe looks down and starts moving around. Next thing I know, one of the working girls pops up from under his desk, wiping her mouth.

"Get out of here and go get ready," he tells her.

When she walks past me, she strokes my chest, but I grab her hand and pull it away from me. "Don't touch me." She shrugs her shoulders and exits the office. "I thought you weren't going to touch the girls?"

"Free pussy, man. They're whores. They're not going to get attached. What's up?"

"Why is Carrington here, and why is she working the rooms?"

My face stays impassive, but I'm holding on by a thread. One of our waitresses quit after last weekend because one dickhead cornered her and tried to shove his hands up her skirt. Carrington is extremely popular. This could go bad really fast.

"I don't want her dancing until her wrist is completely healed. These idiots renting the rooms are willing to pay top dollar to have our featured dancer working the room. She's agreed to doing lap dances, thank God, and she's getting to keep all of the tips and percentage of the room."

This does not make me happy. Too many things could happen to her. Blow and alcohol are a bad combination

"Who's working security in the room?" I don't want to seem too eager, but dammit I need to be in there.

"I figured you should be in there, but I do have a couple of guys coming to talk to me on Sunday. They'll be hired strictly for the back rooms. If you can, I want you to be here to feel them out."

"I can do that. Just let me know what time. I'm going to head back out to the floor." I stand up and make my way toward the door, but his voice makes me stop.

"I've been impressed with the extra stuff you've been doing for us. We've got big plans, brother." He dismisses me, and all I want to do is tell him that

I'm not his fucking brother.

Back on the floor I find Bridgette talking to Carrington. God, I hate the way she's always touching some of the girls. I know she's bisexual because last night Tucker and a dancer I hadn't met yet disappeared into her office, and by the noise it was obvious what they were doing, but I don't trust her. I had her run through the system, and there is no one by that name. Bridgette Bishop is a fucking ghost.

***

She's trying to punish me. Carrington has the jackasses in this private room eating out of the palm of her hand. The only reason she's doing it is to get back at me for what I did, or at least that's what I've convinced myself of. Carrington is flirting up a storm and smiling wide at each of these motherfuckers. She's down to her skimpy bikini top but still has the skirt on. I don't know if she's blocking out the fact that the guy next to the one she's giving the lap dance to is doing blow or that in the corner one of the guys is getting a blow job, but she's acting totally oblivious to it.

When the lap dance is done, the prick shows a wad of cash into her skirt and tries to hold his hand there, but before I can do anything about it she leans forward and says something and the guy backs off. It's not until she moves to stand next to me that I can feel a weird energy coming off of her. I look down and see her good hand is clenched so tightly her knuckles are white. I can see her chin is wobbling, but you wouldn't notice unless you got really close to her.

I lean down until my lips are against her ear. "Are you okay?"

She bites her lip hard and stares at the guy who now has a whore against the wall, fucking her. Her head barely moves, but it's obvious she shook her head no. Carrington seems to be losing it. I grab her good hand and ignore her refusal to come with me and drag her out of the room.

Rex, one of my team, is standing in the hall. "She needs some air. We're going out back."

Neither of us says anything, but as soon as the back door shuts behind us, she rips her hand away from mine and shoves me.

"So what? Are we whores now? Is that what you were doing, sampling the goods first? You can't make me do it!" She reaches up and shoves me again but immediately cries out and grabs her wrist.

"Baby, are you okay?" She jerks away from me.

"Don't call me baby. Damien, I'm not a whore. I won't sleep with anyone for money." Big, fat tears spill from her eyes. I reach out and wipe them away.

"I wasn't sampling the goods. The whores and drugs are a new thing they're doing. No one expects you to do it. You are so far from a whore, it's not even funny. I wanted you, Carrington, because you're beautiful, sexy, and so funny."

Her chin wobbles, and I just want it to stop. She stares up at me with those blue eyes of hers, and my heart fucking stutters in my chest.

"Then why didn't you call me or text me back? You just left." She hangs her head. I know I'm such an asshole.

I bend down so my head is next to hers and speak quietly. "There are things—fuck, there are things you don't know, things I wish I could tell you, but I can't. Trust me, you staying away from me is for your own good."

Carrington doesn't say anything to me. She just shakes her head, moves around me, and heads inside. I stand there for a minute, trying to get my shit together. How did this get fucked up? I know how. I never should have touched her, but now that I've had a taste, I want more.

With reluctant steps, I head back inside and find Carrington coming out of Rafe's office with his arm around her. Every inch of me is ready to attack him if he tries anything with her. I follow behind them as they head toward the front. Rafe leans down, whispering in her ear. Carrington smiles up at him and then heads toward the dressing room.

"What's up?" I ask when I move to stand next to him.

"Hey, man. Her wrist is starting to swell up, so I'm sending her home. I gave her her portion from the room. I'm going to go check on some stuff. Will you make sure she makes it out to her car safely?" He doesn't even give me a chance to answer before he's heading down the hall.

I make my way toward the dressing room and wait for Carrington to come out.

Chapter Eleven

Carrington

The minute I step inside my apartment, I rush down the hallway, stripping out of my clothes. I crank the hot water and step inside the stall.

"Fuck!"

I forgot to take my brace off. I toss it on the floor. The tears begin to fall as I think about the shit I saw tonight. Sure, I used to smoke weed sometimes, but not anymore. I hate coke. Coke was one of the drugs that Abby had been abusing a lot when she was self-medicating.

God, I've always been free with my sexuality, but that woman in the room tonight was a whore. I'd seen her give two blowjobs and then let that dude fuck her right out in the open. Shit, then there was Damien and his whole 'there's stuff I can't tell you' bullshit. He's probably married—I gag at the thought. I've never been a homewrecker, and I won't be one now.

I scrub my body and carefully wash my hair.

Stupid wrist. When I finish, I step out and dry off. My wrist is throbbing, so I throw on my robe and make my way into the kitchen, where my pain pills are. I shouldn't have pushed Damien, but damn, I was so pissed at him.

I guess I was good enough to bang until he was done with me. Why does it hurt so much, dammit? I grab my bottle of water, an ice pack, and head back to my room. The pain pills will knock me out, so I crawl into my bed and rest the ice pack on my wrist. It isn't long until my eyes drift shut.

It's eleven in the morning when I wake up. My wrist feels better, but I still slip the brace back on. I go through my morning routine and throw on some yoga pants and a t-shirt. In the kitchen, I scrounge for something to eat and find that I'm in desperate need of groceries.

Grabbing my purse, I decide to go see my parents before heading to the store. Maybe they'll take pity on me and feed me. A short time later, I pull into the driveway of my parents' home, the home I grew up in. The three-bedroom ranch is full of memories, some good and some bad, but I wouldn't change any of it. I open the front door and call out, but I don't hear anyone. The slap of my tennis shoes echo on the hardwood floors as I move through the living room and into the kitchen.

I find my parents sitting on the deck. My mom's feet are in my dad's lap while she reads her Kindle and Dad reads the paper. Luke and I have been so lucky to have two parents who love each other so much. Sure, they fight sometimes, but the fights never last long. The coffee smells heavenly, and I grab myself a cup.

"Hey, guys," I say as I close the sliding door behind me. "Sorry to just stop by without calling, but I wanted to see you."

My mom gets up, smiling as she comes toward me. "This is a wonderful surprise, baby girl." She wraps her arms around me, and I do the same. "You feel too thin. Are they working you too hard? Come inside and I'll make you your favorite breakfast."

When my mom steps back, my dad grabs me and pulls me into a hug. I hug him back, and then he sees the brace on my hand. "What the hell happened?"

"It's just sprained, Daddy. I was at work and an unruly patient bumped into me and I fell. It's okay, it's getting better."

"What the hell. Don't they have security in that hospital?"

I hate lying to him. God, I fucking hate it, but I hopefully only have to work there a bit longer. If my dad shows up at the hospital, not only will he find out I lied, but my coworkers will find out that I'm a stripper, affecting what they think of me.

"They do. They took care of it. The patient had to have an IV and he was afraid of the needle."

That seems to appease him for the time being. "Where's Wukey?"

"He went with Joe and Parker to the batting cage."

My brother and cousins are the only boys, and they're all close in age so they're just as close as I am with Abby, Violet, and Lilah. I sit down at the breakfast bar, and my dad sits next to me. My mom starts moving through the kitchen and whips me up my favorite breakfast from when I was little. Dad wraps his arm around my shoulders.

"How are Grandma and Grandpa doing?" My dad's parents are so awesome. My grandma still runs the bakery that she started when my dad was young. Grandpa retired from the business he owned with my mom's dad when I was in grade school.

"They're good, but they'd love to tell you that themselves." He gives me a wink, but it's true I need to stop by and see them. My brother and I are the only grandchildren that live close to them. My uncle Jason's kids live on the west coast.

"I promise I'll try to get over there this week to see them." My mom sets a plate of scrambled eggs with maple syrup on them in front of me. "Thanks, Mom, they look delicious."

Yeah, I know my mom's a fitness nut and I'm eating eggs drowned in syrup, but that was the only way she could get me to eat eggs when I was little. My dad shakes his head next to me.

"I don't how you can eat that shit. You ruin perfectly good eggs by pouring *that* all over it." He looks at the bottle of syrup in my hand.

I give him a big cheesy smile as I shovel a forkful of eggs into my mouth. Dad just shakes his head and goes back to reading the paper and drinking coffee.

Mom and I talk about Abby and Ben's wedding that we're helping throw in two months' time. All of us are helping, though. We want it to be magical for her. With everything that's happened, she deserves it and so does Ben and his little girl,

Natalie. Abby asked me to be her maid of honor and of course I said yes. She and I have been thick as thieves since we were little. There isn't anything that I wouldn't do for her, and I know she feels the same.

The trial against Abby's attacker—we don't use his name, because the bastard doesn't have one, as far as I'm concerned—starts next week. The idiot pled not guilty, so now Abby has to face him. As a family, we all plan on being there even though I know we'll have to listen to her talk about what happened. Though I've heard it before, it's still hard. I know my parents are worried about Uncle Dylan because when the guy was being escorted out of the hospital after the most recent attack, Uncle Dylan went after him. Luckily, Aunt JoJo was able to stop him from doing something that could get him arrested.

I know they're concerned that Uncle Dylan or even Ben would go after the guy again, but I think they'll keep themselves in check for Abby. As I finish my eggs, my mom hugs and kisses me before heading out to meet with a client. Once I'm done, I rinse my plate and stick it in the dishwasher. I refill my coffee cup and then my dad's and sit down.

"You doing okay?" he asks. "You seem sad, baby girl."

"Daddy, I'm fine. My wrist hurt me last night, so I had to take a pain pill. They make me groggy. I promise I'm fine."

I hope he believes me. He doesn't need to know that the man I was beginning to fall for stopped talking to me and is being a secretive asshole. Oh well, there's no use worrying about it. In a little over a month, I'll hopefully be out of The Thirsty Beaver and working at the hospital, doing what I want to do more than anything.

I don't stay much longer, and I let my dad know that I'll go visit my grandparents soon. I head to the grocery store. As I push my cart through the store, I grab the necessities. While looking at the fresh produce, I feel eyes on me. I stand upright and look around. No one seems to be looking at me. Maybe it's just paranoia after thinking about Abby's ordeal and it's got me jumpy.

I start looking through the tomatoes when the hairs on the back of my neck stand up. Again, I look around, and this time I spot a man staring at me. He's too far away for me to get a good look at him, but he looks familiar. I grab my tomatoes and quickly move down the aisle. Very quickly, I rush through the rest of my shopping. I glance around as I stand in the checkout line.

After I pay, I push my cart out quickly to the parking lot. I'm just to my car and loading the groceries into my trunk when that creepy sensation comes over me.

"Pepper?" I freeze and look behind me.

My old English teacher stands behind me with a skeezy smile on his lips. *Great.* He's seen me dance. After quickly shutting my trunk, I turn around and keep my back to my car.

"I don't know what you're talking about."

He moves toward me until we're almost touching. My pulse speeds up, and I just want him to go away. "Don't lie, I've seen you. You're beautiful when you dance—you know that, right? I come watch you all the time. I like to sit in the corner and imagine that you're dancing just for me."

My stomach turns as I try to figure out how to get him to go away. In high school, I thought he was so hot, but the way he watched us girls was unsettling. I'd blown it off at first, but then he'd casually start touching me all of the time.

I don't know if he ever tried the shit he did with me with other girls, but I can only assume he did, and who knows how many actually took him up on his offer. With steps backward, I move toward my door, but with every step I take, he moves too.

"Well, it's only temporary. My boyfriend has been wanting me to quit," I lie, but he doesn't need to know that. Quickly, I climb into my car, shutting and then locking myself inside. He bends down until his face is in my window.

"I can't wait to see you dance next time. Maybe I'll pay to get one of those lap dances." He stands up and walks away.

My hands tremble, and it causes me to fumble with my keys as I try to stick them in the ignition. I don't dare look in the direction that Mr. Travis went. I don't want to see it if he's staring at me again.

I want nothing more than to call my dad and tell him that Mr. Travis is messing with me again, but then my dad would find out that I'm dancing and that's the last thing I want. I feel like I need to tell someone.

With shaky hands, I pull my phone out of my

bag and scroll through my contacts. Damien's name pops up on my screen, and I hit the phone key. My hand trembles as I hold the phone to my ear.

"Hey," Damien says, his voice sounding thick with sleep.

"Damien." The tears begin to fall as I tell him about what just happened, and by the time I'm done talking, I have hiccups.

"Baby, where are you?" I tell him the name of the grocery store. He tells me that I'm not too far from his place. "Are you okay to drive?"

"Yeah, I-I think so." I'm starting to calm down a little.

"Come to my place, okay?"

I agree and hang up. With a deep breath, I put my car into reverse, back out of my parking space, and then put the car into drive. Sure enough, I'm ten minutes from his place. When I pull into a parking spot, I see him walking toward me. If I wasn't still a little freaked, I might admire the low-slung pajama bottoms and his muscular chest on display for me.

Quickly I open the door, scramble out of my car, and run to him, not even caring that, at the moment, I'm still pissed at him. He wraps his arms around me and hugs me tightly to his chest. He smells like warmth, musk, and sleep, and I find it unexpectedly comforting.

"Go inside and let me grab your groceries."

He kisses me on top of my head. I make my way toward the door to his apartment and step inside. Damien follows behind me with my bags of groceries. "Let's just put these in my fridge for now." We work side by side to put everything

Evan Grace

away.

When we're done, I don't really know what to do with myself, so I just stand in the middle of his kitchen. He wraps his arm around my shoulders and leads me into his living room.

"Here, sit. I have to make a call, but I'll be right back."

He hands me the remote to his TV, and I watch his retreating form as he disappears down the hall.

***

Damien

I shut my bedroom door behind me and pull my work phone out of my nightstand. I call Hector, my boss at the agency. He answers, and I ask him to look into Jackson Travis. I don't trust the piece of shit. The creep has targeted my woman twice now, and I don't like it. *Shit.* I shake my head. She's not mine.

"This guy approached her in high school?"

"Yeah, she was a junior. Her dad went up to the school and made such a stink the guy resigned. She hasn't seen him since, but apparently he's been showing up at The Beaver and watching her dance. He told her he imagines she's dancing for him. I'm afraid this could escalate quickly."

I didn't tell Hector that I've been intimate with Carrington because I don't really want to hear the lecture about her affecting my focus on the case. Things are moving along, and I feel like if I hold out just a bit longer, I'll get a break in the case, but

108

I'm very aware of that fact that Carrington could affect my work on this case.

"I'll dig around and see if we have a reason to pick him up. For the time being, I'd tell her to keep an eye out for this guy." I thank him and hang up.

I scrub my face with my hands before getting up and heading back into the living room. Carrington is where I left her. Sitting down next to her, I wrap my arm around her shoulders and pull her into my side. She sighs and snuggles into me. I'm not sure what she's watching, but I'm just enjoying the feel of her next to me. It doesn't take long before my eyes feel heavy, and I rest my head on top of hers.

My eyes open, and I don't know where the fuck I am. It takes a minute to realize I'm on my couch, alone. Maybe Carrington went to the bathroom. I stand up and stretch, my back feeling stiff from sleeping on the couch.

"Carrington?" I call out, but I hear nothing. Outside I look and see that her car is gone. I open the fridge and see that she grabbed all of her stuff.

On the counter, I see a folded piece of paper with my name on it.

Sorry to have bothered you earlier, but thanks for letting me hang with you for a bit. I promise not to bother you again.
Carrington

"What the fuck?" I mutter. "She's not going to bother me again?"

Great, she's got me talking to myself. Of course,

what did I expect? I blew her off and was a dick. I just can't believe she actually came to me in the first place, but I'm sure it's because her parents don't know that she's dancing and she doesn't want them to find out.

One thing I know for sure is that I'll be talking to the rest of my security team at the club so that they can be on the watch for the douche bag if he tries to come to see Cari again. This is one more thing that I need to worry about, but I'll be damned if I let that creepy fucker anywhere near my girl.

Chapter Twelve

Damien

It's been a week since the incident with Carrington, and I haven't heard from her at all. I've called her and texted her, but all of my calls and messages have gone unanswered. I know she's okay because I've driven by her place. This past week she's been with her family every day at the courthouse. I did a little investigating and found out they were there for the trial of the man who had sexually assaulted her cousin.

The guy is obviously an idiot because he opted for trial by judge. He's more than likely going to go away for a long time, but it's what the piece of shit deserves. It's likely the guy is going to be sentenced within a week.

Unfortunately, Hector was unable to find anything more than a couple of complaints about Jackson Travis. Tonight I made my team aware of the guy and gave them his description. They know to keep watch for him, especially since Carrington is dancing tonight.

I walk down the hall after leaving Rafe and Tucker and spot Carrington standing by the DJ booth talking to Casey and showing him a CD case. She's animated as she talks to the kid who looks at her like she hung the fucking moon. The kid nods his head and then takes the CD case.

Carrington's lips move, and I can tell she's saying *thanks* to him. She flounces away and comes toward me, but instead of stopping to talk to me she keeps moving. I follow after her, but I stop when I notice Tucker watching me closely.

Moving toward him, I give him a chin lift. "What's up?" I ask him.

"Are you guys fucking? Because it looks like something's going on." Tucker doesn't seem pissed, just curious, but there is no way that I'm going to confess to anything, especially something that has to do with her.

"Nah, she's sexy as fuck, but I wouldn't go there."

I slap him on the back and walk away. My hope is that Tucker believes the shit I just spouted.

An hour later, the club is hopping and drinks are flowing. I do a sweep of the club for that fuck to make sure he's not here, lurking in the corner. For now, he hasn't turned up, but I won't stop watching because I know he'll show. Carrington's already been out to dance once, and I don't know if anyone else could tell, but I could tell that she was nervous. Her eyes kept darting around, and even though she smiled while she danced, she did it shakily.

Rafe and Bridgette are talking in the hallway by

the party rooms when I do my hourly walkthrough of the club. I give them a chin lift as I walk past, but Bridgette stops me with a hand on my arm.

"What's up?" I ask.

"The prick messing with Carrington hasn't been spotted, has he?"

Bridgette was very vocal about us making sure the guy didn't get in here. I'm not sure if she's involved in all the shit that Rafe and Tucker are in to, but she doesn't mess around with the girls' safety, and I give her props for that.

"No, he hasn't. I've been making sure to check the darker corners of this place. I don't know how far he'd actually take things, but he approached her in the parking lot of a grocery store and messed with her when she was only sixteen. I have to believe that he'd take things pretty far now." I'd be damned if I let him touch her. "I want to be notified if anyone requests her for a lap dance."

They both agree that she'll be watched more closely, especially if she gets a request for a lap dance. I leave them to whatever they were talking about. Earlier tonight they had me go collect money that was owed to them from a party last week that somehow got shorted. I had to rough the shithead up, which I hated, but I had to make it look legit just in case Rafe and Tucker were having me followed. Plus, the prick should've known better than to short us for services rendered.

In my gut, I know someone else is pulling the strings, and that's what I've been trying to figure out. I just can't figure out who it is and how deep this all goes. These guys are so tight-lipped about stuff, so this case is taking longer than anticipated.

The night has been pretty uneventful, or as uneventful as a night in a gentleman's club can be. Every time Carrington comes out to dance, I feel myself tense up. She is so sexy and beautiful when she dances, especially since I've seen her really dance. Her body has really leaned out since she came here, so she's lost some of her curves, but her tits are still gorgeous, full, and perky. The other men watch her dance, and you can see the lust in their eyes. I hate it.

The two lap dances she's done were fine. Just a couple of assholes wanting my girl to rub against them. She's finished her last dance for the night, so anytime now Carrington will be heading out this way, and my plan is to get her to come back to my place so we can talk.

I know she may put up a fight after the shit I did, but there's no denying the chemistry we have. In all reality I should take her ignoring me as sign that I should just say fuck it, but dammit I don't want to. Yes, when she finds out that I've been lying to her she may dump me anyway, but at least I'd get her for a little bit.

The secrets I'm keeping from her are for her own good and safety. I know she's kept it a secret from her family that she didn't pass her boards and is dancing until she can take them again, so we both have them. Do I see a future with this girl? I don't know, but honestly, I want to find out.

Not too much time passes before I spot Carrington walking out from the hallway. I watch her go to the DJ booth and hand some cash to

Casey. That's one thing I really like about her. She's quick to take care of others.

Casey hugs her and then she heads to the bar, where she hands some cash to Taylor. Every time Carrington does this, Taylor tries to refuse. They squabble back and forth for a while and then finally Taylor hugs her and takes it.

Carrington comes toward me. "Can you have someone escort me out?"

Like hell I'm gonna let someone else do it. With a hand to the small of her back, I give her no choice but to let me lead her out to the parking lot. We step out into the cool night, and neither of us says anything at first. She opens her back door and throws the bag in, and when she shuts it she looks at me.

"You can go back in now."

"Have you seen the prick at all?"

"N-No, I haven't. Thanks again for being there for me." She opens her door, but I stop her from climbing in.

"Wait."

She freezes and turns to face me. I shouldn't do it, but I grab her face and kiss her lips. She doesn't respond at first, but then I feel Carrington open her mouth and her tongue seeks out mine. I move until she's pinned against her car. This is a mistake, someone could see us, but right now I don't care. I reach down and grab her thigh, lifting it until it hooks around my upper thigh.

She moans into my mouth as I grind my hard dick against the apex of her thighs. I'm so lost in this kiss that it startles me when I hear a door slam.

We pull away from each other, and I look behind me, not seeing anyone.

I turn back around, and Carrington is already shutting her door. She starts her car and pulls out of her spot. She doesn't even give me a second glance as she drives away from me. I'll let that go…for now, but I need her. She's under my skin. We'll just have to play it smart. I hate the fact that we'll have to hide, but it's what needs to happen right now.

I step back inside and find one of the dancer/whores, Cherry, standing at the mouth of the hallway. My fists clench as a sick feeling comes over me. She's one of the last people I'd want to know about Carrington and me. Cherry got really mad when I first came here to work and wouldn't fuck her. She came on to me hard and fast. She may be hot as fuck, but she's sleazy and manipulative.

I take a deep breath as I approach her and say nothing—just giving her a chin lift.

"I saw you." I freeze at her words.

"Pardon?"

"I saw you practically fucking Carrington against her car. I thought you didn't fuck the help?" I don't like the little twinkle in her eye.

"I don't. I don't know what you think you saw, but you obviously missed me pushing her away after *she* kissed me." I'm not sure how much she exactly saw, but I'll play this fucking game all night long with her.

"Hmmm…maybe, but it didn't look to me like you were wanting to push her away. I honestly don't see the appeal, though. She's okay looking, but you could do so much better." She tries to be

116

sultry and sexy, but it comes across as jealous and desperate.

"Oh, I could do better? I think anyone would be better than someone who jumped at the chance to spread her legs for cash." Cherry's hand comes up to slap me, but I grab her wrist, stopping her. "Don't even think about it. You made that choice, not me. As far as Carrington goes, she's a hundred times the woman you are, and she doesn't have to spread her legs either."

I leave her where she stands, kicking myself the whole way. I may have just made things a lot harder for both Carrington and me.

***

My sister waves to me from the table she's sitting at. We share the same DNA but couldn't look anymore different. I have dark hair, hazel eyes, and I'm tall. She has blonde hair, brown eyes, and is a pixie. I dwarf her.

"Hey, squirt. Thanks for inviting me to lunch."

She gets up from her seat and wraps her arms around my waist. I kiss the top of her head before we both sit down. She's in college, studying to be a veterinarian technician, so she's always studying.

"I feel bad I missed your birthday. I know you can't talk about it, but how's work?"

"It's work. What about you? How's school? Last time I talked to Mom, she said that you had some big exam coming up."

Growing up, Victoria struggled in school. She was in every available therapy they offered in school. They helped her with her reading, math, and speech, and, with a lot of hard work, she managed to graduate on the honor roll.

"Yeah. I had a midterm exam on Radiology and Parasitology, and all of the studying paid off because I aced it," she says, her lips tipping up in a huge smile.

"That's great, but I don't know what the fuck you just said."

Her laugh makes her sound like a hyena, and it makes me smile. I've always felt the need to protect her ever since we were younger. It was partially due to her small size, but it has always been in my nature to protect others.

We order our lunch, and she tells me about a guy she's dating. It's funny that she won't tell me his name because she knows I'll run him through the system to see if he's been in trouble with the law. She eventually will have to introduce the guy to our parents, and then our dad will call me and give me the prick's name.

The waitress brings our food, and we both dig in. While eating, a group of women walk by us and sit at the long table across from us. We pay them no mind and continue to eat. I feel Victoria's foot hit me under the table. I raise my eyebrow in question. Her eyes motion to the table of women. Trying to appear casual, I glance to the side and see Carrington staring at my sister and then me. She tries to hide it, but I see the hurt flash through her eyes before she turns her head and starts talking to one of the other women with her.

"Who is that?" my sister asks.

"She's no one." I say it louder than I intended, and out of the corner of my eye, I see Carrington get up from her chair and then head toward the door.

"That didn't look like she was no one. Are you with her?"

At the other table, I watch the older woman who looks like an older version of Carrington get up and follow her out as my sister talks.

"V, it's so complicated. I can't talk about it, but yes, I'm with her or at least I was."

Out the window, I can see Carrington and I'm guessing her mom talking across the street. The sun shines down on her hair, making her auburn waves shine like the most beautiful sunset. I want nothing more than to go to her, but instead I stay in my seat.

A few minutes later, I look back outside and see Carrington loop her arm through the other woman's and head back toward the restaurant. I turn back to my sister, who is watching me with a dopey grin on her face. If this whole situation gets back to my mother, which, knowing Victoria, it will, Mom will want to call me and find out what's going on. What are the chances that Carrington and I would end up in the same place?

I grab our check and stand up, choosing to ignore my pesky little sister but not stopping myself from looking at Carrington, who is looking down at the table, probably to avoid looking at me. Tonight, neither of us works, so maybe I'll just show up at her place and say…what, I don't know, but we should talk at least.

I walk my sister to her car, hug her, and tell her goodbye. I watch as she pulls away. On my way back to my place, I begin to think about what I want to say to Carrington, but of course, that's if she'll even see me.

Chapter Thirteen

Carrington

"Hey, what's wrong? You've been quiet since lunch."

I turn and look at Abby. Surprise doesn't cover what I felt when we walked into that restaurant today and I found Damien there with a girl who was gorgeous. They looked to be really into each other. I don't want to admit that it hurt to see him with someone else. My plan had been to just ignore them until I heard him say, *"She's no one."*

After that, I had to get the hell out of there. I was surprised when my mom came out to talk to me. Of course I had to lie to her and tell her I just need some fresh air because I got really hot all of a sudden. When we finally went back inside, I looked at the table until I knew he was gone.

"Nothing's wrong. I'm just tired. I swear, working third shift sucks sometimes. I'm off for the next two days, so now I have to try and stay up so I get on a better schedule, only to go back to my third shift schedule later in the week." Abby grabs my hand and gives it a squeeze. "Sorry, don't mind me. I'm just moody. I think today went well. I can't believe our moms think that we can put together a wedding in less than two months, but you know it'll be great." I hold her hand in mine while we drive toward my apartment. "I love Ben and Natalie, and I'm so glad you have them."

Abby flashes me a quick smile. "I'm so happy, Cari. I swear, sometimes I keep expecting things to fall apart, but then I remind myself that I've been through a lot and I deserve to be happy. Natalie was so upset that she couldn't come today, but Ben is off for the first time in a week so he wanted to take her out for a daddy-daughter day."

I love that Natalie has started calling Abby "Mommy." Their plan is for Abby to officially adopt Natalie after they get married.

We pull into the parking lot of my apartment complex, and I give Abby a big hug before I move to climb out of her car. "Okay, so I'll go try some dresses on and I'll send you the pictures."

Abby's starting back up at school to finish getting her teaching degree. She told me what color she wanted me to wear, emerald green, and to find the kind of dress I want. She already bought her wedding dress, so I know the style I should stick to.

"I love you," I tell her. She says the same, and I shut the door behind me.

Once I let myself into my apartment, I change into sweatpants and a t-shirt before collapsing on the sofa and binge watching a Netflix show about a girl who had been kidnapped and held in a bunker and then how she acclimates on the outside. The comedy is freaking hilarious, but I'm so exhausted. I feel my eyes start to drift shut.

***

I jerk awake at the sound of a pounding at my door. It takes a second for me to realize what the fuck is happening. Once the cobwebs clear from my brain, I walk toward the door. I don't really need to look out the peephole to know who it is. I can just sense it's him.

"Carrington, open the fucking door," Damien says from the other side. I cross my arms over my chest. Do I answer it? Then I'd have to admit that he hurt me earlier, and I don't know if I'm really ready to do that.

He pounds again. "Dammit, Carrington. Let me in so we can talk. I'm not leaving until you open the door, and just so you know, I can pick each of these locks and let myself in if I really want."

This man is insufferable. I stomp toward the door and flip the deadbolts before flinging the door open. Again, I cross my arms over my chest as I stand in the doorway. Ugh, why does he have to be so fucking sexy? His dark hair is all disheveled. He's wearing a dark blue Henley with the sleeves pushed up to his forearms. His tattoos peek out of the top of his shirt and on his forearms. I don't want to admit that I'm getting all tingly at the way he fills out his jeans.

"Are you going to let me in?"

He leans against the doorjamb, and I either want

to climb him or kick him in the balls.

"Fine. Come in," I huff and walk toward the kitchen. I hear him close and lock the door. "What do you want? I think you made things pretty clear earlier when you told your girlfriend I was no one."

I grab my bottle of white wine out of the refrigerator and pour myself a generous glass before I turn around to face him.

What I don't expect is for him to start laughing, and I mean grab-his-belly, throw-his-head-back laughing. "I don't think it's very funny, asshole."

He tries to get his laughter under control while I shoot daggers at him with my eyes. "Victoria's my baby sister. We haven't seen each other in a while due to both of our busy schedules, so we met up for lunch. I'm twenty-six years old. She doesn't need to know my business because then my mom needs to know my business and honestly I didn't know what to tell her, so I lied." He walks toward me until we're almost touching, and he wraps his hand around the back of my neck. "It's nice to know that you were jealous."

I roll my eyes and try to push him away with my good hand, but the man is solid and unmovable. His thumb brushes against my chin as I stare up at him.

"I wasn't jealous. I honestly didn't care." I freeze for a second, and something occurs to me. "I thought you said you were an only child."

"I lied. I don't let a lot of people in so I don't do a whole lot of sharing, but yes, I have one sister, Victoria." I want to ask him to elaborate, but I don't.

"Is there anything else I should know about

you?"

He shakes his head and tips my head back. I feel an ache deep in my belly as he leans down. His lips brush against mine. I should push him away, I should tell him to leave, but instead I wrap my arms around his shoulders and let him pick me up. My legs immediately wrap around his waist, and my back meets the wall.

My tongue licks at the seam of his lips, and before I know it, he's taking control of the kiss. His tongue duels with mine, and he sucks it into his mouth. I feel it when he begins to move through my apartment, and he doesn't stop until my back hits my mattress and he's on top of me. I welcome the weight and feel of him on top of me.

Maybe this is a mistake and maybe I'll regret it later, but I don't care right now. I just want to feel him inside of me. Damien's lips move down my chin and then up to my ear. Goose bumps break out all over my skin as he licks and then nips at my earlobe. He lower his lips, kissing down my neck. He grabs the hem of my t-shirt and pulls it up over my breasts until it's off. Damien unhooks the front of my bra and my tits pop free for his mouth to latch onto my nipple.

I cry out and arch my back as he sucks and nips at the hardened point. With his other hand, he tweaks and twists the other. He alternates between the two until my breasts and pussy ache. His lips begin to move again, this time down my stomach. I feel him untie the drawstring of my sweatpants and slowly and methodically push them down my legs.

"You are so fucking beautiful. I want to drown in

you," he whispers as he kisses back up my legs. "Spread 'em, baby." He grabs my thighs and pushes my legs open wide. Damien leans forward, and I can hear him breathe me in. I swear I have a mini-orgasm. "Mmmm…you smell delicious." He begins the sweet torture of licking and sucking me.

I grip Damien's hair, and my hips move as his tongue lashes against my core. Moan after moan rips from my mouth as I feel his thumbs spread me open and he tongue fucks me. He sucks my clit into his mouth as he thrusts a finger inside of me. I cry out and then moan as he rubs his finger against my g-spot. The pressure builds as he continues to assault my pussy. Every lick, every suck, drives me closer and closer to coming.

A whimper leaves my lips as he pulls his finger out of me, but then I cry out as he pushes two back inside of me. He taps on my g-spot over and over as a pressure unlike anything I've felt before starts to build inside of me. I'm so wet that I can feel my juices running down my ass. Damien sucks my clit into his mouth, and in seconds I detonate. I come so hard my back arches up off of my bed, and I grip his hair so hard that I've got to be hurting him, but I can't bring myself to care.

He licks and sucks at me as he brings me down from my climax. Damien kisses his way up my body and hits my lips. I can taste myself, and I moan against his mouth. I grab his shirt by the hem and pull it quickly over his head as he undoes his pants. He barely gets them down before he's thrusting his huge cock inside of me. Again, my back comes off of the bed, and I cry out. Will I ever get used to his huge dick being inside of me? I'm so wet that it helps as he begins to thrust in and out of me.

He grabs onto my headboard for leverage as he drives in deep. "You feel that, baby?" he whispers, his voice thick with a sexiness that makes my core clench. "You feel how deep inside of you I am?"

"Yes, oh God, yes! Fuck me hard, make it hurt!" I'm so delirious right now. I've never felt so much pleasure.

Damien grabs one of my legs and pushes it back, giving him access to hit me deeper than before. That tiny bite of pain makes me cry out incoherent babble. He pulls out of me, flips me over, and pulls me up by my hips before he thrusts back in and begins pounding me with punishing strokes.

"You feel so good, baby. So tight and so fucking wet. I'm going to make you come so hard." His large body drapes over mine. He wraps one arm around me and strums my clit.

He wraps his other arm around me until his hand is around my throat and his lips are on my neck. I feel the ball inside me tighten up until it explodes, and I come with a shout and a cry.

"Oh fuck, baby. You're squeezing my dick so hard."

He groans against my skin before grabbing both of my hips again and pounding into me over and over and then planting himself deep as I feel him begin to pulse inside of me.

I sigh as Damien kisses down my back before slipping his softening cock out of me, and then I collapse onto my bed.

He moves my limp body around and tucks me close to his body. He wraps his arms around me, and I feel safe and loved, but I don't let myself believe it. Damien's hiding something from me. I can feel it.

His lips touch the back of my head, and I sigh. I roll over to face him and kiss his neck, tasting the slight saltiness of his skin, and then I snuggle in close.

"Damien, what's going on at the club? Things seem to be changing. I don't want to work those back rooms ever again." I say this all in a whisper. Being in the back room while the men did coke and fucked someone who was clearly a prostitute made me feel ill.

I feel his body stiffen before he relaxes again. "Baby, it's complicated, but trust me. You don't have to work back there. I don't want you working back there. When's your test?"

"Two weeks," I say as my fingers lightly trace his tattoos on his chest. "I've been studying every free moment I've had."

I've passed the two practice tests I've taken, but I passed them before too. If I don't pass, I don't know what I'll do.

"Let me work on a way to help you pass," he says. He tips my face up and kisses my lips slowly and thoroughly. It's not long before I'm straddling him and sinking down onto his length.

***

My body aches as I stretch, and my ass comes in

contact with a hard dick. Very carefully, I roll over until I'm facing Damien. In sleep, he looks younger and not so intimidating. I reach out and stroke his cheek with my fingers. His face is rough with stubble, and the sound of my fingers rubbing against his cheek echoes in my room. What are we doing? Is this just sex? We haven't really been on a date. I haven't introduced him to any of my family, but he hasn't either.

I've had casual sex, I've had one night stands, which I'm not exactly proud of, but I've never slept with someone for this long and without defining what sort of a relationship we have. Do I ask him what we are? Or do I just take it for what it is? Last night was incredible, and I can already tell I'm going to be sore, but I welcome it.

I slide out of bed and throw on my robe. In the bathroom, I take care of business and then brush my teeth. On my way to the kitchen, I throw my hair up into a messy bun. While the coffee is brewing, I pull out some eggs and bacon and get breakfast going.

I'm just scrambling eggs when Damien wraps his arms around my waist and kisses and bites at my neck. "Mornin,' baby." His voice is thick with sleep. I turn in his arms and kiss him quickly before grabbing him a cup of coffee. He drinks it while leaning against the kitchen counter.

"Are you working at the hospital tonight?"

"No, I actually didn't sign up for any shifts for the next couple of weeks so I could study. Why? Do they need me to dance tonight?" Ugh, I hope not. I've made a lot of money, but if shit is starting to get bad there, I want out, and as quickly as possible.

"Uh, no. I wanted to see if you wanted to go out tonight." I'm taken aback, especially since he looks nervous asking me.

"Yeah, sure. What'd you have in mind?" I ask as I scoop eggs and bacon onto our plates. I carry our plates while he carries our coffee out into the living room. We sit side by side as we eat.

"I thought maybe dinner and then we could go play some pool or something."

"Okay, that sounds like fun. What should I wear?" Oh, I already know what I'm going to wear, but I want to hear what he wants.

He places his empty plate on the coffee table and turns toward me. Damien reaches out and winds a strand of my hair around his finger.

"Baby, you could wear a burlap sack and you'd still be beautiful. Just wear whatever you want." He kisses my cheek. "I've got to get going. I've got shit to do, but I'll be back to pick you up at seven."

He disappears down the hall, returning a few minutes later fully dressed. I stand up and walk with him to the door. He grabs me, and his mouth crashes down on mine. His tongue enters my mouth, dueling with mine. He grabs me by my ass, pulling me toward him, and swallows my moan. All too soon, the kiss is over, and he's walking out my door.

As I clean up my kitchen, I think about Damien. There is so much I don't know about him. I know he's keeping stuff from me, but why? I'm hoping tonight I get to learn more about him. I mean, I know we get along and we have lots of sexual chemistry, but I want more. The truth of the matter is that I am starting to have major feelings for someone I hardly know and someone who has been so hot and cold with me. What I do know is that he's so easy to talk to—I've never told anyone about my insecurities when it comes to my parents.

Damien is just very easy to talk to. I hope tonight goes well because I want this to go somewhere, and I hope that he does too.

***

I slip the diamond studs that I got for my graduation from my grandparents into my ears. My hair hangs down right below my bra strap in big waves. My eyes are smoky, making the blue of my irises pop. I gave myself dewy cheeks and covered my lips with a red gloss. In the front, my dress looks modest. It's a black scoop neck, long sleeve mini dress that hits a little higher than mid-thigh, and when I turn around the back is open all the way down to my lower back. Thin strips of fabric criss cross the back to hold it up and together.

My spiked heels have laces that wrap up my leg, ending mid-calf. I feel so sexy when I wear this dress. Unfortunately, this is only the second time I've worn it. I'm just throwing my powder and lip gloss into my clutch when there's a knock at my door. I quickly spritz some perfume on before rushing toward the door.

When I open it, I freeze. Damien's standing in front of me in a white dress shirt with the sleeves rolled up to his forearms, showing off his beautiful ink. His shirt is even tucked into a pair of dark blue jeans, and of course he's wearing his black motorcycle boots.

I look up at him, and he's staring at my legs.

"How do I look?" Stepping back, I give a little twirl, and when my back is to him, I hear him moan. "What? Don't you like it?"

He wraps one of his arms around me and brushes my hair back from my neck. He buries his nose in my neck. "You look fucking beautiful, and you smell heavenly. Let's go before we don't leave at all."

Grabbing my wrap for me, Damien drapes it across my shoulders and, with a hand to the small of my back, he leads me out to his Jeep. We're both quiet as we drive toward Charleston, but it's a comfortable silence as we listen to the music on the radio. We pull into the parking lot of a Mexican restaurant, Los Agaves. He parks and tells me to wait while he comes around to open the door for me. As we make our way inside, he wraps his arm around my shoulders and mine winds around his waist.

The hostess seats us at a booth toward the back. I sit across from Damien, and he grabs my hands from across the table. Our waiter brings our chips and salsa, I order a margarita, and Damien orders a Dos Equis.

"What did you do after I left today?" He lets go of my hand to grab a chip and dips it into the salsa. I do the same, popping the salty, hot goodness into my mouth.

"I studied for a bit and then took some cupcakes over to my grandparents' house. What about you? I know you said you had 'shit' to do."

Our waiter interrupts us. We both order beef enchiladas. I take a huge sip of my margarita. "Well?"

"I had to do some stuff for the club, and then I had to get my bike ready for storage." He drinks some of his beer. "Tell me more about your family."

"Hmm…okay. I have a younger brother, Luke, and he's almost eighteen. He's heading to LSU this summer for baseball. He's really super talented. My mom has two brothers, twins, Dustin and Dylan. Uncle Dylan and Aunt Journey have four kids. Abby is the oldest, then Joey, Parker, and then Haddie. Uncle Dustin and Aunt Stacy have three girls: Violet, Lilah, and Daisy. My dad has an older brother, Jason, and he's got four kids: Grace, Maisy, Tucker and JJ. They live in Washington."

"Wow, that's a big family."

"Yeah, and they're all crazy, but I love them like mad."

Just then, the waiter places our plates in front of us, and we both order another drink.

Conversation is light as we both dig into our meals. I love that when I talk, Damien shows genuine interest in what I'm saying. We talk about our favorite music, and I think he's surprised that I love bands like The Dirty Heads, Sublime with Rome, Stick Figure, and Slightly Stoopid. He, of course, is a huge fan of rock: Metallica, Disturbed, Volbeat and classics, like AC/DC and Black Sabbath.

"My dad is a die-hard Metallica fan. Always has

been," I tell him.

We finish our dinner and our drinks, and Damien pays the tab. I excuse myself and head to the bathroom. I touch up my lip gloss. In my clutch, I grab a mint and pop it into my mouth, chewing it while I fluff up my hair. I head back out and find Damien standing at the entryway to the bathrooms. He again drapes my wrap around my shoulders. Hand in hand, we head out to his Jeep. He opens the door for me, and I climb inside, buckling my seatbelt as he shuts the door.

"Tell me about your sister." I turn in my seat, or I turn as much as I can with a seatbelt on.

"She's younger than me. Her name's Victoria, and she's going to school to become a vet tech."

Getting him to talk about personal stuff is like trying to pull teeth.

"Are you guys close? What about your parents? Did you grow up around here?" Ugh, I should've stopped after that first margarita. They tend to give me loose lips, and this will just scare him off.

He chuckles as we pull into the parking lot of the bar, Rascal's. He turns toward me. "Yes, we're close. Yes, I'm close to my parents, and I grew up in Charleston. Any other questions?" I shake my head. "Do you want to play some pool?" I nod, and he pulls me to him. His kiss is soft and tender and makes my toes curl. Again, I wait for Damien to come around and help out.

Hand in hand, he leads me into Rascal's. I've been to this place a few times. Damien heads toward the back, to the pool tables. For a Wednesday night, the place is actually hopping. A waitress comes and takes our drink order, and if she doesn't stop eye fucking Damien I'm going to take off my heels and hit the bitch with them. After she disappears, he wraps his arms around me. The ass is chuckling.

"Oh, you think that's funny? Do you think it's funny that the guy by the dart boards is staring at my ass?"

It's almost comical how fast Damien whips his head to the side and spots the guy I was referring to. He shoots him a death glare and stands to his full height, trying to look as intimidating as possible, which is easy for him to do.

The waitress brings our drinks while Damien racks the balls. I grab myself a pool cue and the chalk. Damien grabs his own stick and joins me.

"How about a little wager?" he asks. Little does he know that I've been playing pool with my dad since I was twelve.

"Okay, what are the stakes?" I'm curious what he wants to play for.

"Hmmm…how about whoever wins gets to call all of the shots in bed for one night? It means whoever wins gets to do whatever they want." He says that last bit very slowly. I'd love to dominate this man just once. First, I've got to school this fool.

"Deal, but first can we play a warm-up game? I haven't played in a while." I'm hoping that my smile is innocent as I look up at him.

I let him break them, and he sinks a solid. Back and forth we take turns. I've scratched twice on purpose and have even let him "help" me a couple of times. Every time he sinks a solid, he looks at me with an arrogant smile. I keep sipping on my drink and biding my time until I can beat the arrogance right out of him.

He ends up winning, which I let happen. We order another round, and he hands me money for the jukebox. I move to walk away, but Damien stops me and pulls me to him. He wraps his arms around me. "I need a kiss first." He dips me a little and kisses me hard on the lips. "Go play some tunes, baby."

Damien slaps my ass as I walk away. I can't wait to kick his ass at pool, and I smile all the way to the jukebox.

Chapter Fourteen

Damien

I should be racking the balls, but I can't take my eyes off of Carrington. All night that fucking dress has tortured me. I've never seen a more perfect female form. Her legs are long and lean, if not leaner than when she first started working at The Beaver. She's got a luscious ass on her. She must've gotten it from dancing. Some song about sirens comes on, and she dances her way back toward me.

Her lips tip up at the corners as she gets closer. Carrington's eyes sparkle under the lights, and the blue stands out more. The closer she gets to me, the more something warms inside of me. She's got me all twisted up inside. When she's within grabbing distance, I grab her hand and pull her to me. I cup her face and stroke my thumb over the light dusting of freckles on the apple of her cheek.

My lips brush against hers with a light touch. I pull back and whisper, "Are you ready to get your ass kicked?"

"Bring it on."

She sways her hips as she walks to the table, grabs her stick, and breaks. In that moment I know I've been played. In a matter of minutes, she's sunk half of her balls.

By the time I'm even with her, she's using distraction tactics—bending over the table but making sure her ass is sticking out, walking by me and rubbing against me. Back and forth, we battle it out, and I start using my own brand of distraction. Every time she's up, I move her hair off of her neck, kiss her neck, and let my hand drift down to her ass.

It's finally down to the eight ball and my shot. Carrington stands next to me, and I hear a clatter.

"Oops, I dropped my stick," she says in a high-pitched, breathy voice. I can't help but watch as she bends at the waist and grabs her stick off the floor. Of course it makes her butt stick out more, and all I want to do is grab it, damn her.

"I know what you're doing, and it won't work." I line up my shot, but it misses the pocket by barely an inch.

"Oh no! You missed." She walks around the table to take the most perfect shot I could've left her.

She sinks it with barely a tap. I burst out laughing when she starts busting a move while singing, "I won," over and over. She's got the attention of most of the bar, and she looks fucking adorable. Carrington finally dances her way right toward me. She wraps her arm around my neck and smiles up at me. "I'm seeing you tied to your bed while I torture, tease, and torment you. Has anyone ever tickled your prostate before?"

Fuck no, but why does it turn me on to think of her doing that to me? My dick is so hard right now, and if we weren't in public, I'd throw her down on this pool table and fuck her...hard.

"Jesus Christ, Carrington. What the hell is this?"

I freeze and feel Carrington do the same. Her father and a dark-haired gentleman are standing at the other end of the pool table, looking at her with narrowed eyes.

"Hey, Dad," she says slowly. Her back is to my front, and I can feel a slight tremble. "Hey, Uncle Dylan. What are you guys doing here?"

Her dad walks toward us, his lips turned down into a frown. "Don't you think it's a little inappropriate to dress like that in public? Jesus, can't you just once not act like this?" I hear her swift intake of breath and wrap my arms around her waist. He looks up at me. "Who's this?"

"Um, this is Damien. Damien, my dad, Luke Carter." I step around Carrington and reach out my hand. He reluctantly reaches out and shakes my hand. She goes to her uncle, and he wraps his arms around her. Every thing is so awkward right now, but I suppose if I had a daughter I'd react the same way, but probably worse.

Her dad pulls her into a hug, and whatever he whispers in her ear makes her go ramrod straight. "You're right, I'm sorry," she says.

She stands by me. "I'd like to go home now."

I wrap an arm around her waist and guide her

outside after she says bye to her dad and uncle and help her into my Jeep. She's quiet, and I can feel the distance between us. I grab her hand, lacing our fingers.

"Baby, tell me what he said that upset you."

She stares out the window and at first won't say anything.

"He said I should watch how I dress and act in public because it may give someone the wrong idea."

I bite down on my tongue to keep myself from saying the shit I want to about her dad. What kind of man says something like that to his daughter? "He's wrong. You know that, right? You're sexy, but more than that, you're confident. There is not one goddamn thing wrong with being confident enough in yourself to show off your body."

She looks at me with a look of surprise on her face. "Um, uh, thank you for saying that. We've always butted heads when it comes to how I dress. He obviously hates it. If he had his way, I'd be dressed like a nun. It's frustrating. He makes me feel like a slut." She hangs her head as if she's ashamed.

We get back to her apartment, and I help her out of my Jeep and walk with her up to her door. I want to stay, I want to hold her and make that look disappear from her face, but she might need the space.

"Do you want me to stay? We don't have to do anything. I just want to be able to hold you."

"I'd like that." She unlocks her apartment, and I follow her inside, locking the door behind me. I watch her set her clutch on her dining room table before heading toward her bedroom. "Help yourself to a beer," she tells me before disappearing into her bedroom.

I grab a beer out of her refrigerator and carry it into the living room. Carrington's door opens a few minutes later, but she hurries across the hall to the bathroom. When she finally rejoins me a few minutes later, her hair is up in a bun and her face is sparkling clean. Instead of sitting next to me, she climbs right into my lap and buries her face in my neck. My arms automatically wind around her. Neither of us says anything. I just take a minute to appreciate and enjoy the feel of her in my arms.

Carrington yawns loudly against my neck. "Come on, baby. Let's get you to bed."

I stand up with her in my arms and carry her back to her bedroom. She lets me lay her down and then watches as I strip out of my clothes. I crawl in next to her, grab her, and twist her around until she's draped over half of my body with her head on my shoulder.

"I'm sorry I ruined the rest of our night," she says against my skin.

"You didn't ruin anything. Your dad was wrong, you know. I think he stills sees you as his little girl. If I have a daughter someday and she looked like you, I'd probably be the same, if not worse. Better yet, I'd probably lock her away until she was forty." She snuggles in closer to me.

"Thank you for saying that. I'm actually used to it. He hates the way I dress and act. He always has. I'm sure he wishes I were a boy or that they wouldn't have lost my sister, Rose. She probably would've been perfect."

With that, she rolls over and her soft snores fill the room. I know I'm a guy and all, but she kind of just broke my heart.

I move so my front is against her back, wrap one arm around her, and tuck my other arm under my pillow. It doesn't take long before I feel sleep pull me under.

***

A week has gone by since our date, and Carrington's been acting like everything is okay, but I know different. I can see it in her eyes at times, but she just brushes it off. We've spent just about every day together, and I've learned two things. One, I've started falling for her. The second is I've fallen for her...hard.

I can't wait for her to take her test, which is in a week. Every time I have to watch her dance, I feel myself get homicidal. It sucks to see the look of lust on all of these different men's faces. Some of the other dancers and working girls have started treating her worse than before. I'm sure it has to do with Cherry and her big fucking mouth, and now I think Bridgette is starting to get suspicious of us, but so far she hasn't said anything.

I don't think they would care, but if what I'm doing gets out, they could go after Carrington, and that's the last thing I want. That's why I should've stayed away from her, but I can't anymore. Two nights ago, we went to the movies and since it was a

Tuesday night, we were the only ones in the theater. Thirty minutes into the movie, I had Carrington in my lap and my tongue in her mouth.

We ended up dry humping like a couple of teenagers, but damn if it wasn't fun. I took her back to my place afterward and fucked her hard against my bedroom wall. The girl is a wildcat, but she attacks sex the way she attacks everything, with passion and vigor.

I pull into the parking lot of a little hole-in-the-wall bar outside of Savannah to meet my handler. We only meet face-to-face monthly. I give him the latest information I've got. My handler's name is Toby. We've both been with the DEA for a couple of years. He got injured pretty badly in his last field assignment, so now he works a desk and has been my handler since I went undercover.

Inside, the place is perfect for a meet: dark and loud enough that we can't be listened to. I spot Toby in the corner and make my way toward him. I've always been a big guy, but next to him, I feel small. Toby has blond hair and blue eyes, and he's around six foot six and at least two hundred forty pounds of solid muscle. He stands up and gives me a back slapping hug that I return.

I sit down across from him and wave the waitress over. We order a couple of beers, and once she brings them we dismiss her so we can talk.

"So, how's it going?" Toby asks.

We both take a drink and I set my bottle on the table. "I'm making some progress. The deliveries and pickups have gone well, but I know it's all a test. These are low-level dealers. So far, it's just

Rafe and Tucker who speak to their supplier. The prostitution is what is worrying me. The girls not involved are getting uncomfortable with it, but so far they're not getting pressured to turn tricks. Two of the dancers—Cherry, real name Michelle Lang, and Diamond, real name Rochelle Marie, are both sleeping with customers for money. They've kept a tight lip on the whores they've brought in. I haven't seen money exchange hands, but I will. Here is the info on the two dancers."

Toby takes the piece of paper from me. "We'll watch them and see if we can pick them up outside of the club. We don't want the brothers getting suspicious. Anything else you want me to take back to the office?"

"No, I'm hoping to have more information for you soon. They have cameras everywhere, so taking pictures is impossible. Rafe and Tucker have changed their schedule a bit, so I'm trying to figure out how to get in there to see the security feed. If I can just get cash exchanging hands on video, that would be enough to make them squirm, mess up maybe."

We finish our beers and plan to be back here in a month unless something big happens before that.

On my way home, I decide to stop by my parents' house. Even though my mom and I talk on the phone, I think she likes seeing my face just to know I'm still alive. I was twelve when my dad was shot in the line of duty. It had been so hard, even at that age, watching my mom break down. She's always been strong and supportive of our career choices, but that was the one time I saw her lose it.

Dad had been called to a robbery in progress and the perp open fired on him. It caught him by surprise, and he took one to the shoulder. The perp was just a kid, sixteen years old and desperate for money to feed his family.

As upset and sad as Mom was when it happened, she supported Dad's decision to help the kid get a reduced sentence. I don't know whatever happened to him, but I know he didn't serve all of his jail time.

***

The club is hopping tonight, and there's a weird vibe in the air. I'm not sure what it is, but I don't like it. No one else seems to notice. I ask the other bouncers to keep an eye on the crowd and the dancers, and I always make sure two guys are back by the private rooms. I'm not taking any chances. Leaning against the bar, I scan the crowd, giving Rafe a chin lift as he walks by.

Bridgette meets Rafe in the mouth of the hallway, and they disappear into her office. They don't let anyone in their offices alone. Otherwise I would've planted a bug in her office. I've planted a bug in Rafe's office, but I never get anything that I haven't already heard or been told.

It makes me wonder if they're becoming suspicious of everyone and that's why they're meeting in Bridgette's office. Now I just need to get a bug in there too.

I turn back toward the floor and watch the guys all watch the dancer, Fawn, a beautiful African

American woman, twirl around the pole. She's a great dancer and keeps to herself. I've seen Carrington and Taylor talk to her before, and she's always friendly, but not overly so.

Out of the corner of my eye, I spot my girl. She's walking right toward me. We usually try to avoid any interaction because we don't want anyone becoming suspicious. As she gets closer, I cross my arms over my chest and try to school my features and look bored. She stands next to me, close enough that her arm is brushing mine. The flowery scent she wears wraps around me. I'm addicted to that smell, especially when my face is buried in her neck.

"Hey," she says, and it's almost too quiet to hear.

I turn so I'm facing her. She looks beautiful. Her hair hangs down in russet waves, and her eyes are done in a glittery, smoky look that makes the blue stand out. Her lips are painted the most enticing deep pink. She's already been out to dance once, so she's wearing a silver glittery string bikini. My cock is trying desperately to get hard, but I'm fighting it every step of the way.

"What's up? You know us talking isn't a good idea," I tell her. Her eyes clench shut tightly, and I regret the harsh tone I've used.

She shakes her head and says forget it and walks away as fast as she can. Carrington is making me want to fucking claim her in front of everyone, but fuck, it's a bad idea. I hate the hurt look on her face before she walked away. She disappears toward the back.

Brett, one of the guys working the private rooms,

approaches me. "Have you seen Pepper? There's a guy that wants a private dance, and he wants her."

"She went down the hall. Who's the guy?"

I really hate that she does private dances, but again, I can't stop it or they'll suspect something.

"I don't know, some Hispanic guy with a wad of cash." At least it's not the fucking teacher. I've been diligently watching for him, and he hasn't shown up.

"Okay, I'll send Taylor back to get her."

Five minutes later, I see Carrington walk out from the back in a tiny skirt and the sparkly bikini top. She meets Brett at the mouth of the hallway and disappears down the hall.

Then, in a matter of minutes, shit falls apart.

Chapter Fifteen

Carrington

I don't want to do this damn lap dance. This is, by far, the worst part of the job. Almost every time, the guys try to get me to dry hump them and want me to feel their erections. It grosses me out and makes me feel dirty. Luckily, security is never too far away from me.

Brett leads me toward the private rooms, and all I want to do is walk right out the door and never come back. I could. I've made enough money that I've got some savings. My boards are in a week, and I feel more prepared than I did before.

Damien is standing where I left him just a little while ago, and I try not to look at him. It really hurt me earlier when he was so cold and standoffish. I know we were supposed to keep our "relationship" quiet, but it's starting to make me feel cheap and like I should be ashamed or maybe that he's ashamed of me.

At the mouth of the hall, I feel a sense of

foreboding and my steps falter. I shake it off because I'm just being silly. I take a deep breath and shake out my hands as I move toward the room. The rooms for the private dances don't have doors, only curtains, and that's a good thing because if there is trouble then security can reach the girls quickly.

Brett pulls back the curtain. "Remember, asshole, don't touch her unless she gives you permission."

I step into the room and the curtain closes behind me. The guy is standing in the middle of the room. A baseball hat obscures his face.

"Hey, there!" I say with fake enthusiasm. He moves closer to me, and I finally see his face. I move to take a step back. "What are you doing here?"

"I want you to dance for me, Carrington."

Jackson Travis starts stalking toward me. I'm frozen in my spot until he's almost to me, and then I move. There's a lot of yelling out in the other part of the club, and before I can reach the curtain, he wraps his arm around my waist, pulling me until my back is against his chest. He grinds his erection against my ass, and my stomach starts to roll. I open my mouth to scream, but he covers my mouth with his hand.

My heart beats a rapid staccato in my chest. His lips touch my ear. "I've waited such a long time for this. I only wish that asshole father of yours was here to see what I do to his precious daughter." I struggle in his arms, and he just holds me tighter. "I figure we only have a few minutes before one of those meatheads comes in here. I better hurry."

His hand slides up and covers my breast. I'm starting to hyperventilate. He starts dragging me toward the sofa. The heel of one of my shoes breaks, and I trip and fall forward. Jackson tries to get on top of me when I hit the sofa, but I roll off of it onto the floor. On my hands and knees, I scramble across the floor, picking up my broken heel.

He wraps his hand around my ankle and I kick out, catching Jackson in the face. "Fucking bitch!" He grunts. He grabs me by my waist and flips me roughly over onto my back. He tries to climb between my legs, but I kick at him and realize I'm still clutching my broken heel in my hand.

I let him think he's got the upper hand until his face is up by mine. The heel bites into my skin as I grip it tight in my palm. "Don't fight me," he says. I nod my head, and when he brings his mouth down to mine, I lift my hand, bringing the heel down somewhere on his back. He howls like a wounded animal. I wiggle out from underneath him and hobble on my broken heel through the doorway, smacking right into a body.

"What the fuck! Carrington, are you okay?" I look up and see Rafe in front of me.

I shake my head and point to the room. "A-A m-m-man tried t-to attack me!"

Then, in a flurry of activity, Rafe, Tucker and Brett, who disappeared earlier, are all in that room. Bridgette and Damien come rushing toward me.

"What the fuck happened?" Damien grabs me and pulls me up into his arms. I'm taken aback by the tenderness he's showing me, especially since

Bridgette is right with us. "Are you okay? That asshole paid someone to start a fight out on the floor so we'd be distracted. Stay with Bridgette. I'll be right back." He moves me to stand with Bridgette, who wraps her arm around me.

All I hear from the room are raised voices and the sound of someone being punched. A moment later, Rafe comes out, followed by Brett and Damien, who are dragging Jackson out.

"You stabbed me, you bitch!"

Damien grabs Jackson's hair and wrenches his head back. "You want to say that again, motherfucker!"

The men take him toward the back exit and disappear out the door.

"Let's go to my office and get you a drink." I let Bridgette lead me into her office. "Sit, take your shoes off before you hurt yourself."

I sit down on the little sofa and slip my shoes off. A glass with amber liquid appears in front of me, and I take it graciously. I don't even bother sipping it. I just slam it down.

The burn is a welcome feeling, and I hold out my glass for another, which Bridgette pours for me. Again, I slam it down, clenching my eyes closed. I feel the burn of tears. I bite my lip to keep from crying out, and it works until Damien walks in and I'm up and running toward him. With my arms around his shoulders and my legs around his waist, I bury my face in his neck and begin to cry.

"Shh…baby, it's okay." He starts moving toward the door. I hear Rafe asking Damien what he's doing. "I'm getting her the fuck out of here."

151

"Cari, we'll talk tomorrow. I'm sorry that happened, and I promise it won't happen again." I look at Rafe through tear-filled eyes and nod my head before burying my face back in Damien's neck.

Damien places me in the passenger seat of his Jeep and straps me in. I lean against the door, resting my forehead on the cool glass. The Jeep starts up, and then Damien places a jacket over me. I realize I'm still in my little bikini and no jacket. The scent of leather and Damien wraps around me, and between that and the two huge shots I had, I feel my eyelids droop. I welcome the sleep that overcomes me.

***

My eyes flutter open, and it takes my mind a while to wake up enough to figure out where the hell I am. Last night comes back to me. Damien wouldn't tell me what they did with Jackson, but I could feel the anger radiating off of him in huge waves. When we got back to his place, he had gently woken me up and carried me inside, right to his bedroom, laying me down on his soft mattress.

"I'll be right back," he whispered against my lips.

I snuggled into his blankets and felt myself slip back under. The feeling of his lips on my neck woke me, and then Damien's softly whispered words were breathed against my ear. "Is this okay?"

Something inside me warmed at the thought that he was sweet enough to ask me if it was okay for him to touch me. I grabbed his hand, pulled it around to the front of my panties, and shoved them inside.

He'd made love to me, nice and slow. When I came, it was intense.

My body aches as I roll over and find Damien's side of the bed empty. It's cold, letting me know he's been up for a while. I slide out of bed and gingerly walk to Damien's dresser. Grabbing a t-shirt, I throw it on. It's huge on me and hangs down to right above my knees. I step across the hall to use the bathroom and splash cold water on my face.

As I stare at my reflection, I can't help but smile. Damien sure did his best making me forget about last night. My eyes are bright, my lips swollen, and there are whisker burns on my neck. I brush my teeth with my finger before rinsing my mouth. The smell of coffee and the sound of Damien's voice entices me as I make my way down the hall.

"I want him picked up and thrown behind bars." There's a pause. "Yeah, I got it. I know. I won't compromise anything." Another pause. "We'll talk soon. Bye."

I'm assuming he's talking about Jackson, but what could be compromised? I step into the kitchen and go right to the cupboard to grab two mugs. Today I need the extra boost of sugar, so I put cream and four sugars into my mug and a splash of milk into his.

I turn around as Damien comes toward me. He pulls me so my body is flush against his. With his lips against mine, I sink further into him. His fingers move up into my hair, and he tips my head as he inhales me. All too quickly, he pulls away, but he rests his forehead against mine.

"How'd you sleep?"

"I slept great, thanks to you." Even with everything that happened last night, I still smile up at him. "Um...you do know that they probably know about us now, right?" I wasn't thinking when I decided to jump him. Plus, he's the one who always takes care of me.

"I don't care, because from now on you'll never be without me in that club." He kisses me once more and then grabs his coffee, disappearing down the hall. I'm not sure what I'm supposed to be doing, so I take my coffee into the living room and sit down. After last night, I'm more determined then ever to pass that damn test.

***

Damien pulls up in front of Charleston University and throws his Jeep into park. Today's the day I retake my nursing boards. I bite at my thumbnail as I stare at the entrance.

It's been a week since Mr. Travis attacked me at the club. True to his word, the next night Damien was right there everywhere I went. When I first showed up, I got called into Rafe's office. Rafe, Tucker, Damien, and Bridgette were all sitting in there, waiting for me. For a split second, I assumed I was going to be fired. I figured I was becoming more trouble than I was worth.

Instead they were beefing up security for all of the girls, and due to the knowledge they now had regarding Damien and me, they were going to leave him to my personal security. They all talked about me, about us, like I wasn't even in the room. Damien promised them that our relationship wouldn't affect either of our jobs. I honestly don't know why I even bothered showing up.

When it was over, they dismissed us. Damien threw his arm around my shoulders and led me out to the floor. As soon as Taylor had spotted us, she gave me the biggest, dopiest grin. The rest of the night went off without a hitch.

I finally got to meet Taylor's boy, Grayson, the other day. He's so freaking cute and doesn't look anything like his mom. He's six but tall for his age. His hair is blond and long, and she had it up in the most adorable man bun. His eyes looked almost silver. We had met for lunch and took him to the park. Grayson's dad was Taylor's high school boyfriend who split as soon as he learned she was pregnant.

Her parents threw her out, but her favorite aunt, who never married, took her in and helped with Grayson. They didn't live with her anymore, but they still lived close so she was able to help with him when Taylor worked.

After our lunch date, I love Taylor even more. She's so funny and smart, and it's very obvious that she loves her son to the moon and back. After my lunch date with her, I spent a couple of hours searching for my maid of honor dress. Since it was going to be cooler out, I chose a dress that came with a wrap. The dress was emerald green, per the bride's request. The style was like Abby's dress, a form-fitting bodice with a full skirt, but mine ends at my knees. The top has capped sleeves, and the dress has a beautiful lace overlay.

For shoes, I bought a pair of silver sparkly strappy heels that were going to look killer. Abby tried to tell me that she was going to pay for my dress, but that was not going to happen.

Once that was taken care of, I buckled down and studied like crazy. Damien made flashcards for me and quizzed me over and over. I swear that even in sleep I was dreaming about the questions.

"Babe?" Damien's voice pulls me back to the present. "You're going to do great. Text me when you're done, and I'll be back to get you." He pulls me toward him and kisses my lips hard. "You got this."

I bit my lip and then take a deep breath. "Thank you for everything."

As I step out onto the sidewalk, I close my eyes and take a deep breath before making my way inside. My steps echo as I walk down the corridor to the computer lab, where the test is being given.

Sweat starts to dot my forehead as I see my room up ahead. I take a second to take a deep breath and clear my head. *You can do this, girl,* I think to myself over and over. I remind myself that if I pass this test, then I am that much closer to quitting The Beaver. When I reach the room, I grab my paperwork and driver's license, handing them to the older woman sitting behind the table.

She points out what computer is mine, and I grab my chair and have a seat. Again, I close my eyes, clear my mind, and begin.

Secret Love

***

Damien

Carrington just texted me and told me she was done and ready for me to pick her up. I look at my phone. It's only been an hour. She said last time that it took her two hours to take it. This is hopefully a good sign.

While she was doing that, I met my mom for lunch. Of course, Victoria told Mom about Carrington, so I fessed up. She spent a good ten minutes chastising me for lying to Carrington about who I am, not bringing her to meet them, and asking question after question about her.

Before my mom would let me leave, I had to promise that I would bring her around and they would call me by my middle name and my undercover name, Damien. I don't like asking my parents to lie to her too, but for now it's what's best for everyone. Pulling up in front of the entrance, I spot her walking toward my Jeep. Her face is unreadable as she opens the door and hops in.

Her chin wobbles as I watch her, and I hate seeing her cry so I grab her and pull her across the console until she's in my lap.

"Hey, why the tears? Did it go bad?"

"N-No, but what if I fail it again?" She wraps her slender arms wrap around my neck. I wipe her tears away.

"When do you get the results?"

"In forty-eight hours, I can look up a preliminary report to at least see if I passed or failed, but I still

157

have to wait six to eight weeks for the official results before I can work as a RN."

"Okay, so we have two days before there's anything to be worried about."

We head back to my place. After making dinner together, we sit down in my kitchen and dig into our steaks, baked potatoes, and salads. My girl digs in to her food with vigor. When we're finished, we work side by side cleaning up the kitchen. I'm wrapping up the last of the food when I feel her arms slide around my waist.

"Thank you for being there for me today. No matter what, I will be forever grateful for your support."

Her lips touch the middle of my back, and I honestly feel my heart skip a beat. I turn around and wrap my arms around her, hugging her close. I don't know how I thought I could stay away from her. Oh sure, in the beginning, it was purely physical, but there is just so much more to her. She's smart, caring, and compassionate. When she spoke of her family, she did it with so much love.

Her need to seek the approval of her parents worries me, though. I don't know how much of her need for approval is her parents' doing or her just assuming the worst. Her dad clearly loves her, and his reaction at the bar was probably just his overprotection of her. Now, do I agree with how he handled it? No, but someday when we have a daughter—where the fuck did that thought come from?

I kiss the top of her head. Her hair smells like raspberries, and I want to stay there with my nose buried in her hair. Instead, I kiss her forehead and tell her to go pick out a movie on pay-per-view. The truth. I need to tell her the truth. If there is any hope for us to work, I need to tell her who I really am. It's risky, but I trust her to keep my secret. As I throw the popcorn into the microwave, I make my decision. I'll tell her after she gets her preliminary test results back.

Minutes later, popcorn in hand as well as two sodas, I make my way into the living room and find Carrington cuddled up under a blanket on my couch. "What'd you pick, baby?"

"I got the new Leonardo DiCaprio movie you said you wanted to see."

I pull the blanket up and sit down next to her. She cuddles right into me as she reaches into the bowl for a handful of popcorn. Once we start the movie, she moves in closer to me and I wrap my arm around her shoulders. As the movie starts, I lean back because Carrington has maneuvered herself so her head is resting on my chest.

Not even twenty minutes into the movie and I already know that she's asleep. I'll let her sleep for a bit before I wake her and take her to bed. I sift through her hair as her soft breath hits my chest. She was just supposed to be a fuck, nothing more, but damn she's becoming so much more than that. She's becoming everything, and if I lose her I don't know what I'll do except fight like hell to keep her.

***

"Eyes, baby," I murmur against Carrington's lips

as I slowly sink my cock inside her.

After the movie was over, I gently woke her up and watched her sleepily stumble into the bathroom and then across the hall to my bedroom. Quickly, I picked up the trash and locked up. When I made it back to my room, I found her curled up under my comforter, fast asleep.

I had stripped down into my boxer briefs and slid in beside her, immediately pulling her against me.

I'm not sure what time it was when she woke me with her lips against my neck and my dick in her hand and hard as a rock. After that, I took over, devouring her lips and moving between her thighs.

Now, as I bury myself to the hilt inside of her, something shifts between us. Even in the dark of night, I can feel it. It's warm and sweet, and damn I want to stay inside her forever. She reaches out and cups my cheek. She strokes my skin with her thumb, making my dick jerk inside of her. I move my head to kiss the pad of her thumb, and I thrust slowly.

Together, we move, and her soft moans and cries echo in my bedroom. My breathing sounds rough and loud in my own ears as I feel her channel squeezing me. "That's right, baby. Squeeze my cock." I bend down, sucking her nipple into my mouth, nipping at her hardened bud. Every time I nip at it, her pussy squeezes me.

"Damien, I'm so close."

I grab her thigh and pull her leg up higher, hitting deeper inside her. Carrington grips my shoulder so tight that I can feel her nails digging into my skin, possibly cutting it. I release her nipple with a pop, reach between us, and rub her clit. My lips attach to hers as I feel her clench around me. With every thrust, I give a little grind, hitting her sweet spot and making her cry out against my mouth.

I pinch her clit and hold deep as she begins to come hard. She cries against my mouth, and her hips shoot up off of the bed, almost throwing me off of her body. With a strong grip on her hips, I pound into her over and over again.

"Fuck, baby. Milk my cock." I bury my face in her neck as the tingly sensation travels down my spine and shoots from my balls straight up to my cock. I grunt against her neck.

Carrington wraps her arms around my shoulders and holds me tight. She rubs her fingertips softly against my skin, and she whimpers as I pull out of her. I realize that I didn't use a condom.

"Baby?"

"Hmm..." she mumbles, her voice sounding sated. I rest my forehead against her stomach, kissing her smooth skin.

"I came inside you. I promise I'm clean. I'm so fucking sorry, and I've never done that before. Are you protected?"

Her fingers sift through my hair. "I'm clean too. It's been a while since I've been with anyone, so I'm not on any protection. The timing should be right that pregnancy wouldn't happen, though."

I move my hand up her chest, over her breasts, and up to her face.

"Okay, but I'm here if it does."

I tell her I'll be right back and grab a washcloth

to clean her up. Then I tuck her in close to my body and feel her drift off to sleep, drifting off right behind her.

Chapter Sixteen

Carrington

My laptop taunts me as I sit in my living room, staring at it. It's been forty-eight hours. Well, actually fifty-two hours since I took my boards. I can get online and, for a small fee, I can at least see if I passed or not, but I'm scared. Damien had to work at the club tonight, so he can't be here, but I wish he were.

Things have changed between us over this past week. We've gotten closer, and I'm falling in love with him. I'm not stupid, though. I know he's keeping something from me, but I don't know what. I keep trying to get the nerve to ask him, but I'm scared. What if it's something bad? I know he's the muscle at The Beaver. It wasn't lost on me the night that Mr. Travis attacked me that Damien was the one to beat him up. His knuckles were red and swollen afterward.

He's made comments about things I can't know. Between the drugs and the girls, I don't know how

163

much he's actually involved in, but it worries me that he's heavily involved. What if they get busted and he goes to jail?

I shake off those thoughts because there is nothing I can do about it right now. With a trembling hand, I grab my laptop and pull it into my lap. Pulling up the website, I plug in my username and password and then put in my credit card information. The little icon spins around, and I cover my eyes. I'm afraid to look, and I really wish Damien were here so he could tell me whether I passed or not.

"Come on, Carrington. Stop being a little pussy. Just look."

Slowly, I peel my hands away from my face as my heart starts to pound. I glance at the screen, and a surprised scream leaves my lips. "I passed," I whisper as the tears start to fall. Now I just have to wait six weeks until I get the official letter and then I can apply for a job at the hospital.

I send my boss at the hospital a quick email to let her know that I passed and that I'll be applying for a position as soon as I get the letter. She responds almost immediately that they have a .8 position that is still open, which means I'd work three-twelve hour shifts every week and every other weekend, but it's also considered full-time so I'll get benefits and start accruing paid time off.

I pull out my phone and send a quick text to Damien, asking him to come over after he gets done at the club. How do you thank someone who believed in you more than you believed in yourself? I have one thought that is kind of naughty. My phone dings, and I swipe at the screen.

Hey babe, I'll come over when I'm done. I should be done by one, is that okay?

It's six now. I can lie down and take a nap, and then get up and get ready. I respond quickly.

That will work.

I hope this means you checked your test results. :-)

Maybe…see you later xoxoxo

Now it's time to put together my plan.

***

The sound of my phone ringing pulls me out of my sleep, and I blindly reach out and snag it off of my nightstand. I see it's my mom and I almost hit ignore, but instead I answer it.

"'Lo," I mumble.

"Hey, baby. Did I wake you? Are you working tonight?"

"Yes, you woke me, but that's okay. I needed to get up. What's up?"

I cover my mouth as I yawn and climb out of bed. My mom starts talking as I make my way out into the kitchen to make a cup of coffee.

"Well, JoJo is throwing Abby a bridal shower and she wanted to know if you could help, maybe plan the games or prizes. She knows your schedule at the hospital is crazy, but she'd love your help. How is work, by the way?"

My stomach clenches as it always does when I have to lie to my family. What is it they always say about lies? One lie ruins a thousand truths.

"It's great, Mom. I'm really happy. I've met someone. We work together, and he's really great."

"Honey, that's wonderful. Is he a nurse, a doctor?"

I'm surprised my dad didn't tell my mom about Damien when we ran into him and Uncle Dylan at the bar.

My stomach clenches again. "No, he's actually in security there. He's a little rough around the edges, but he's so good to me." I take a sip of my coffee as I lean against the counter. "I'll call Aunt JoJo. I'm happy to help with Abby's shower. How are the wedding plans coming along?"

"Wonderful. Your aunt and uncle and Ben's mom have got the tent, tables, and chairs all rented. Your grandma is making the wedding cake, and your aunt Stacy got a line on flowers. It's going to be beautiful and just what our sweet girl deserves."

I couldn't agree with my mom more. Abby, Ben, and Natalie deserve their happily ever after. She informs me that they'll want to meet Damien, and I promise that it'll happen soon...maybe. I just hate to ask him to lie to my parents too. With a promise to call her to set up a date for them to meet Damien, I tell her I love her and then hang up.

With my coffee in hand, I make my way into the bedroom and start getting things ready.

***

It's a quarter after one when I hear a knock. I take a deep breath and open the door.

"Well?" he asks. Of course he looks gorgeous as always in his standard uniform: black t-shirt, which showcases his ink and his muscles and jeans that hug his muscular thighs and his impressive dick.

"I passed."

Damien grabs me, and I wrap my legs around his hips as he attacks my mouth. I feel him start moving through my apartment, but I have to stop him. Otherwise he won't get his surprise. I reluctantly pull back. "Wait, we'll celebrate in a minute. I have things planned."

He gives me that cocky fucking smile of his. "Oh yeah? What kind of things?"

"Well, first, I'm going to feed you. And then…well, you'll just have to wait and see."

I lace my fingers with his as I pull him into my little dining room and then push him down into the chair.

As I move away from him, he wraps an arm around my thigh to stop me. "What's all of this for?"

I try to swallow down the knot that's in my throat. He'll never know just how much his support has meant to me, and even though he tried to push me away, he was still there for me, especially since I couldn't exactly confess to my parents that I failed the first time and am now working as a stripper for the time being.

"I just wanted to say thank you."

167

He pulls me down onto his lap. "Thank me for what?" He cups my face, his thumb rubbing back and forth against my skin.

"Just for being there for me, and for believing in me. It was hard to deal with all of this and not being able to tell my family, but you were there. So, thank you." I wrap my arms around him, hugging him tight. He wraps his arms around me and squeezes me tight.

"You know why, don't you?" My eyebrows draw together as I look into his hazel eyes and shake my head. "I'm falling for you."

His voice is low and rough. At his words, I feel tears prickle behind my lids.

"I've fallen for you too," I reply, my words but a whisper. His lips are on mine, and I moan against his mouth. The timer goes off, interrupting our kiss, and reluctantly I pull away. "I have to get our dinner." He kisses me one more time and then lets me go.

I pull out the baked Ziti and set it on the stovetop. While that cools, I pull the salad out of the refrigerator and the bottle of ranch dressing. I feel Damien come up behind me and look over my shoulder.

"Baby, this looks delicious. I'm fucking starving."

"Good, because there's plenty and I'm sending it home with you."

We fill our plates and sit down at the table. He tells me about the club tonight and that he's glad that I won't be there much longer. "Things are starting to get a little crazy," he says before taking a bite, moaning around his fork.

"I hate it, Damien. I really do. It's not the dancing, I can handle that, but it's the stuff that happens in those rooms. Aren't they afraid that the cops will bust them? I mean, they've got to be watching, right? Even some of the girls are starting to look strung out. Taylor said she's considering looking for a job somewhere else. She says she can't risk getting arrested because it could mean her losing her boy."

Damien is tense. I can see it on his face. His jaw clenches, and his mouth is pinched tight. "How soon can you quit?"

"I can't apply for the nursing position until my official letter comes in the mail, but I've saved some money so I could quit soon and just go work in the ER as an aide until it comes."

He visibly relaxes. He's so serious about wanting me out of there.

"Next time you dance, give them your notice. You need to get out of there. Talk Taylor into leaving too. She'll listen to you." I promise him I'll talk to her, and we finish dinner.

Side by side, we work together to clean up, and butterflies take flight in my belly. I hope he likes what I have planned. He's used to seeing woman dance barely clothed, including me, but what I'm going to do is strictly for him.

While he uses the bathroom, I move the coffee table and place a chair in front of the couch. I place my phone in my docking station and get the music ready. He joins me a minute later. I watch his eyes move around the room and then land back on me.

"What are you up to?"

"Okay, I need a minute to get ready, but I need you to sit here." I grab him by his upper arms and lead him backwards until he flops down in the chair, the wood groaning under his heavy frame. "Don't move."

Quickly, I run into my room. I strip off my clothes until I'm just in a silk and lace bra and panties the color of emeralds that I bought.

I grab the white button-down dress shirt that I bought for this occasion and slip it on, buttoning it up until it's buttoned right at my breasts. On my bed are a pair of black, strappy, stiletto heels. I slip them on and stand up, moving toward my full-length mirror. My hair has that messy, just-had-sex look. Too bad I'm about to cover it. I grab my black fedora off of my dresser and stick it on my head. Quickly, I slap some red tinted lip gloss on and take a deep breath.

Right before I reach the mouth of the hallway, I call out for Damien to hit the play button on my iPhone. The beginning note of "Dangerous Woman" by Ariana Grande comes on through my speakers. I take a deep breath and begin to move.

The minute Damien sees me, his mouth opens. Slowly, I move my hips from side to side as I move my hands up and down my body seductively. I drop down to my knees, moving my hips as I slowly unbutton the shirt. Once it's undone and hanging open, I get up and move until I'm straddling his legs. I smirk internally as I watch him stare at my chest with lust-filled eyes. I grind my hips on his lap as I pull the shirt off.

There's no mistaking the huge erection in his pants. With a finger under his chin, I tip his head up to look at me, bending forward to bite his lower lip. By the time the crescendo of the song hits, my panties are wet and my nipples are hard. He cups both of my ass cheeks, pulling me down hard against him. The song comes to an end, and I smile down at Damien.

"I know you see me dance all of the time, but I wanted to do a dance that was just yours, something that no one else will have." Ugh…maybe this was a stupid idea. He's not saying anything. He's just staring at me. "Okay, it was a stupid idea—"

Damien stands up with me wrapped around him. He moves through my apartment and tosses me on the bed. I watch, stunned, as he rips his t-shirt off. On my knees, I move to the end of the bed, rip open his jeans, and pull his cock out.

My tongue peeks out, swiping at the purple head of his dick. I can taste the saltiness of his pre-come. I swirl my tongue round and round until I open my mouth wide and suck his cock into my mouth. He grabs at my hair as he starts fucking my face.

"Do you like sucking my cock, baby?" I moan around it, and he grabs my hair tighter. "Baby, you're taking me so deep. Your mouth is so hot."

I continue to suck, my head bobbing up and down. I grab onto his balls, massaging them. I hear him grunt, and my eyes drift up to look at him. His eyes are on me, and he looks hungry. "Fuck, baby. I need to be inside of you."

Damien grabs me under my armpits, and then I'm up in the air and on my back. He buries his head between my legs, and I cry out. With every swipe of his tongue, I cry out. He sucks my clit into his mouth and pushes a finger inside of me. I grip his head, and my back arches up off of the bed.

"Oh God!" I cry out. The sound of my wetness echoes through my bedroom as his finger moves in and out of me. I feel the pressure build in my pussy, and know that I'm close to coming. "Damien, I'm so close," I say with a moan.

"Give it to me, baby," he whispers as he sucks my clit into his mouth. With his fingers, he presses on my g-spot. Reds and blues explode behind my eyes as my orgasm pulses through me. My blood roars in my ears, and I'm vaguely aware of Damien putting a condom on. He flips me over onto my knees and thrusts inside of me.

My head flings back, and I cry out as he grips my hips in a punishing grip and hammers into me. The sounds of my moans, his grunts, and wet flash slapping into each other fills the room.

"Touch yourself, baby. Help me get you there."

I do as he instructs, reach between my legs, and strum my clit.

I'm still primed from my last orgasm, so it takes no time at all before I'm moaning into my mattress. Damien's body drapes over mine, and I feel his teeth latch onto the skin on my shoulder as his thrusts become erratic. The moment he comes, he buries himself to the hilt and groans against my skin. I cry out as he slides his softening cock out of me, and I collapse onto my stomach.

I feel the bed move as he gets out of it to deal with the condom, I'm sure. He joins me a minute later and situates us so I'm draped over his body and we're under the covers. I place a kiss right above his nipple as his fingers gently sweep up and down my back.

"Damien?" I'm not sure if he's still awake.

"Yeah."

"I was wondering if you'd be my date to Abby and Ben's wedding? It's in a few weeks. It's a small affair, just close family and friends, but I'd love for you to meet everyone."

All day I've thought about whether to ask him to the wedding or not, and honestly I made the decision to ask him about two seconds before I did.

He kisses my forehead and doesn't speak for a minute. I'm beginning to think we're not completely on the same page. "Yeah, I'd like that."

It's too dark in my room, so he can't see my huge smile. I can't wait for my family to meet him. We snuggle until I feel my eyes get heavy and I eventually fall asleep.

Chapter Seventeen

Damien

The vibe is wrong when I walk into the club. As I make my way back to Rafe's office, I think about this past week. It's been a week since the night Carrington "thanked me". Things are great, but I still need to tell her the truth. I just keep putting it off and off and off. I can't help but be afraid that it could push her away, and that's the last thing I want. Even though we haven't been together that long, I feel like I've known her forever. We have so much fun together. She's a major distraction, but I don't care. Don't get me wrong, I love my job. It's just I love her too.

I figured out that I loved her two days ago. She'd spent the night at my place, and after we fucked on my kitchen counter, I carried her into my bedroom, where she proceeded to fall asleep. When I came back after using the bathroom, I froze in the doorway. Carrington looked like my redheaded angel, and it was like everything fell into place. It was at that moment that I knew I was in love with her.

Carrington's plan was to wait until after her cousin's wedding before she quit at the Thirsty Beaver. I hate it, but I understand. She just wants to have enough money saved that she's okay and able to still pay her bills. Plus, she wants to be able to help give her cousin the best wedding possible.

I knock on Rafe's door, and I hear him holler to come in. When I step inside, I find Tucker and Bridgette sitting across from Rafe.

"Come in, Damien. We've got a major problem."

Grabbing a chair, I sit next to Bridgette. "What's going on?"

"Cherry got picked up by the cops last night. Apparently, she was being watched because she got picked up soliciting some asshole at a club after she left here. We've sent our lawyer to talk to her and see if she's going to talk." I look at all three of them. I can't get a read on them.

"What are you going to do if she talks?" I don't like where this is going, and I hope the stupid, spiteful girl keeps her mouth shut.

Rafe looks to Bridgette and then to me. "We'll cross that bridge when we come to it."

They dismiss me right after that, and I don't argue. They might get suspicious if I tried hanging around to listen to their plan.

Later I'll make some calls to see what I can find out. Stupid bitch getting busted might have to make me move things along a little faster.

***

It's been a week since Cherry got picked up, released, and then suspended for the time being. Rafe and the others have been very tight lipped about her, but now they're more watchful than before. Of course it still hasn't stopped them from renting out the back rooms.

I feel her approach and turn my head to watch Carrington move toward me. She smiles that little smile of hers that I love as she sidles up next to me.

She doesn't hug me or kiss me. She simply bumps her elbow against me. "Hey," she says.

I don't even care anymore, so I wrap my arm around her shoulders and pull her into my side. I brush my lips against her temple and inhale her flowery scent as it wraps around me. She places her hand on my stomach and smiles up at me.

"You looked beautiful dancing up there tonight."

"Thanks, baby. Kyle, can I get a bottle of water?" She looks behind her, smiling at the bartender. Kyle places it on the counter and unscrews the cap. I watch her place the bottle to her lips and take a healthy drink. "I'm going to talk to Bridgette tonight about quitting. Do you think they're going to be mad? What if they fire me? I mean, I've got money saved, but it could take two months before I receive my letter, and I don't want to be broke before I have the job."

She looks up at me nervously. I don't know what they'll do, honestly, especially considering the direction they're going in. Carrington's a big money maker for them.

"They might be upset, but they'll understand. Being a nurse is what you've been working toward.

176

Do you want me to be there when you tell them?" She gives me a small smile and nods her head. "Okay, babe. I'll be there."

***

The rest of the night goes by quickly. Once the girls are done for the night, I walk a few of them out to their cars and then make my way inside. Carrington joins me a few minutes later with a makeup-free face and her hair in a bun on top of her head. She wraps her arms around me when she reaches me and pushes up on her tiptoes to kiss my cheek.

"You staying at my place tonight?" I ask her as I bend down, nuzzling her neck.

"Yep. Unless you want to stay at mine."

We agree to stay at my place, and we make our way toward Rafe's office, hand in hand. Between the two of us, we decided to talk to Rafe. I won't admit to her that I'm a little nervous how they're going to react, but I just have to have her back and everything will be okay.

"Just be firm with them, babe. They may try to offer you more money to stay."

I knock and wait for Rafe to tell us we can come in. Through the door, he mutters, "Come in." I push the door open and we step inside. Rafe's sitting at his desk with a redhead I've never seen before sitting in his lap. "You got a sec?"

"Yeah, sure. What's up?" A person would have to be blind to not see that Rafe's got his hand up the girl's skirt. The girl looks at me, and I can tell she's high. Her pupils are like tiny pinpoints, and she certainly doesn't look like she's all there.

"Rafe, I wanted to thank you for everything you guys have done for me. I've taken my boards and I passed, so I'm officially a registered nurse. I won't get the official later for another month, but I just wanted to let you know that in three weeks I'll be done here." Carrington gets it all out and shoots a smile at Rafe. I put my hand on her thigh to halt her bouncing leg.

"What could I say to get you to stay? How much money do you want? Carrington, you've got a gift. You should use it. Do you really think you're going to make this kind of money working as a nurse?" I don't like the tone he's taking with her.

"Rafe, it's not about the money. Sure, I could make more money here, but being a nurse is what I've always wanted to do. I'm sorry if you're not happy about this, but this is what I want." Damn, I'm so proud of her. Rafe can be intimidating sometimes, but she's holding her own.

Rafe looks at her closely, and I know what that motherfucker is trying to do, but she's not cowing to him. My body is strung tight, but she laces her fingers through mine and gives me a smile.

"Well, okay, then. We'll plan a big party your last night, send you out in style."

Rafe dismisses the girl in his lap and turns to look at Carrington, who tries not to look disgusted when Rafe grabs a wet wipe to clean up his hands. We stand up and make our way out of the club. There are only a couple of weeks to go and then Carrington will be done and hopefully my job will be wrapping up soon.

The DEA is watching Cherry, AKA Michelle Lang, since they released her from jail, but so far she's laying low. We know that she's had limited communication with either of the brothers, but Bridgette has been speaking to her a lot. They put a tap on her cellphone, so it's only a matter of time before we get something.

With my arm around Carrington's shoulders, I lead her outside to her car, opening the door for her. "I'm right behind you, babe. Drive safe." I kiss her lips and then watch her climb in, shutting the door after her.

I climb into my Jeep and follow behind her, pulling into the visitor spot when we pull into her apartment complex. She waits for me next to her car, and I lead her to her apartment with a hand to her lower back. Once inside Carrington heads into the bathroom to shower, and I move toward the kitchen to make her and myself a grilled cheese sandwich.

I'm throwing them on plates when Carrington joins me a few minutes later. "Awww...you made me grilled cheese." She takes the plate I hand her, reaches up, and kisses my lips. "Thank you, baby."

My eyes follow her as she moves to the living room. She's wearing a sexy little black silk robe, and my cock immediately gets hard. A little of her ass cheek hangs out of the bottom, and I just want to take a bite out of it.

Her wet hair is braided and hangs down her back. I shake myself out of my Carrington stupor and follow her into the living room. While we eat, she tells me how the wedding plans for her cousin are going and how she's excited for me to meet everyone. I do hate that she'll be lying to her family about me. I should tell her who I really am and soon.

I'll do it after the wedding. I just have to prove to her that everything that I've shown her is truly me and that the only lie is my name and my actual job. She knows everything else, like when I fell off my bike and broke my jaw when I was trying to do stunts. She knows that I'm a big crime novel reader. She knows that when I was a teenager, I was a troublemaker and used to get into fights. She'll see. She'll see that she knows the real me.

She sets her plate on the coffee table and snuggles in to me. I wrap my arm around her shoulders and kiss the top of her head. With a contented sigh, she falls asleep.

***

I straighten my tie in the mirror, grab my black vest, and throw it on. When I finish buttoning it up, I grab some hair goop and rub it through my hair. I dab some cologne on and go back into my bedroom to finish getting ready. I slip on my black boots, stick my wallet in my back pocket, and slip my watch on.

Carrington texted me her aunt and uncle's address, so I'm meeting her there. Her cousin's wedding starts in an hour with the reception immediately after. I'm a little nervous about meeting her family. I know how much they mean to her, and I'm worried about what they might think of me. Really, I shouldn't care what they think of me, but for Carrington, I do.

When I hop into my Jeep a little while later, I plug in the address on my GPS and make my way to Carrington.

Twenty minutes later, I pull up in front of a beautiful ranch-style home, and just as I get out and shut my door, my breath leaves me in a whoosh as Carrington steps out onto the front porch. Her hair is draped over one shoulder in big curls, and her makeup is classic. I make my way up the driveway, and as soon as I reach her, I wrap her in my arms.

"You look so fucking beautiful."

Her smile is dazzling. "You don't look bad yourself." She strokes my arm. "I love this color on you." My dress shirt is a slate gray.

She grabs my hand and leads me around back, to where a huge white tent is set up. "Wow, this is some set up." We step inside the tent and several men, large men, turn around to face us. Carrington's dad is the first to come over.

"Daddy, you remember Damien."

"Yes, I remember. How are you doing, Damien?" He reaches out and shakes my hand. It's much warmer greeting then last time, but he still looks like he wants to crush me.

"Good, sir. Thanks."

Carrington leaves me to go check on the bride. Her dad leads me toward the others and starts making introductions.

By the time the wedding begins, I've met her mom, who Carrington looks identical to, her

181

grandparents, aunts, and uncles. I met Ben, the groom-to-be, and he seems like a good guy. Once the ceremony starts, I can't take my eyes off of my girl. Her eyes are bright, and her smile is so luminescent as she watches her cousin get married.

After the ceremony, the wedding party steps outside for pictures. I move toward the makeshift bar, order a bottle of Bud Light, and take a drink. A teenager that looks a lot like Carrington's dad moves toward me. "You must be Luke."

"Yeah, so you're dating my sister. How's that going for you? She can be a bit of a handful."

"A handful is putting in mildly. You'll have to share some stories with me."

"Oh, trust me. I've got plenty, like when Carrington—"

His words are interrupted when she comes running up and slaps her hand over his mouth.

"Don't you say a word or I'll kill you." She turns to look at me. "He's a liar, so don't listen to him."

It's so easy to see the affection that these two have for each other. Hell, it's easy to see that this whole family loves each other fiercely. My family is close, but this family takes closeness to a whole other level.

Luke kisses his sister's forehead and then leaves us. She immediately wraps her arms around me. My eyes drift to the bride and groom and the groom's daughter. Knowing what I know about what happened to Abby, you'd never guess it. She looks so happy that I'm surprised she's not floating.

Ben has his daughter in arms and both of Abby's arms are around them. They don't seem to notice anyone else is here. It's not hard to miss that everyone is looking at them with so much love and happiness.

Carrington moves out from under my arm but grabs my hand to go introduce me to the rest of her cousins. There is a shit-ton of them.

During dinner, Carrington's grandma, Ruth, sat next to me and questioned me. She was sweet about it, but I felt like I was on trial until finally her husband came over and told her to stop interrogating me.

"Grandma, leave Damien alone," Carrington says from the other side of me, but she says it with a smile on her face.

I try to follow all of the conversations going on, but there are like five different ones happening simultaneously. Our families are definitely different. Mine is fun, nice, and quiet. Carrington's is loud, boisterous, and loving.

After the bride and groom dance and parent dances are done, the party gets rocking. My girl is shnockered, and I've watched her and her cousins do several "dance" routines. The men in her family must be used to the girls doing that kind of stuff because they all just ignore them, occasionally laughing or shaking their heads at them.

A song that sounds like something Carrington listens to comes on, and she pulls me out to the dance floor. I'm not a dancer, but I'll wing it for her. Plus, she's fucking amazing, so it's not a hardship.

"Are you having fun?" she asks, looking up at me.

"Absolutely. Thanks for inviting me."

I bend down and kiss her as the song comes to an end. We dance a bit more, and then everyone says goodbye to the bride and groom as they take their leave for the night. After that, it's not long before the party dies down. Carrington got a ride there, so she's riding home with me.

She takes me around to say goodbye to everyone. The women all smile and hug me, but most of the men stare me down like they're ready to kick my ass if needed. It doesn't bother me, though. Again, if I ever have daughters, I'll be the exact same way.

Chapter Eighteen

Carrington

Damien grips my hips as I move up and down on his cock.

When we got home from Abby's wedding, he laid me on my back on the sofa and buried his head between my thighs. I gripped his hair and let the sensations wash over me. He worked me into such a frenzy that when he finally stripped us both out of our clothes, I attacked him. After rolling a condom down his length and then getting him where I wanted him, I climbed into his lap and impaled myself on his hard cock.

Damien sucks one of my nipples into his mouth, causing a moan to leave my lips. I'm in love with him. I'm not sure how it happened, but tonight, after dancing with him and watching him with my family, it hit me like a Mack truck.

Butterflies always flit in my stomach when I'm around him. He makes me feel like the most important person in the world. Damien believes in me and has supported me one hundred percent while I studied to retake my boards.

"Grind down on my dick," he murmurs against my breasts. Damien's hands span my hips as he works me up and down on his stiff length. I throw my head back as I feel my orgasm start to build. He reaches down between us with his thumb and strokes my clit. Between me rolling my hips and moving up and down and his thumb on my clit, my orgasm explodes. My back arches, and his name rips from my throat.

"Yeah, that's it, baby. Oh fuck, you're squeezing me so tight." He grabs my hair at the base of my skull and tips my head up. His lips attack mine as he takes me down to the floor, pushes my legs back, and begins to hammer into me. "You're going to make me come so hard," he groans against my mouth.

He pinches my nipples as he hits me so deep I cry out. Damien pumps once, then twice. He stays planted deep as he groans. His cock pulses inside of me, causing aftershocks to wrack my body. When he collapses on top of me, I wrap my arms around him, enjoying his solid weight on top of me. God, he makes me want so many things I didn't think I wanted. It scares me so much because that's giving him so much power—the power to hurt me, to break me.

What if he doesn't feel the same way? What if I'm not enough for him? I mentally tell myself to shut the fuck up and not to even go there. I mean, come on. He went to my cousin's wedding, he met my crazy family, and he didn't run. That's got to mean something. All I know is that I want to be with him.

He tenderly rubs his thumb back and forth on the apple of my cheek. "I love your freckles. I want to kiss every one of them."

If I wasn't already on the floor, I could melt into a massive puddle right now. He moves enough that his softening cock slides out of me, and he moves to his side.

Damien helps me move around so we're facing each other, mere inches separating us. No words are spoken, but we don't need them. I can see the warmth in his eyes and the slight smile on his lips.

"Let's get in bed," he whispers.

He helps me up off of the floor and then scoops me up in his arms. Once he lays me down in my bed, he follows and settles in behind me. His arms are banded around me so tight, but it makes me feel safe, secure.

When I drift off to sleep, those three little words slip from my lips, and I slip into dreamland with Damien's arms hugging me closer to his chest and a smile on his lips.

***

It's been two weeks since Abby's wedding, and things have been amazing. Damien and I have spent every day together, and I never would've guessed that he had a romantic side. Last Sunday night, the plan was for me to stay at his place. When I showed up, he met me at the door, covered my eyes, and led me into his condo.

Evan Grace

"Why are my eyes covered?"

"Babe, no questions. Just let me lead you."

I took baby steps as I let Damien lead me with his one hand covering my eyes and his other arm wrapped around my waist. My tennis shoes made a shuffling sound as my feet hit the linoleum. "Are you ready for your surprise?"

A delicious smell, which I didn't notice at first, hit my nose as I nodded. He removed his hand, and I was frozen in my spot. His little kitchen table was covered with a white tablecloth. Two candles illuminated the table, and roses sat between them in a beautiful glass vase.

"I can't believe you did this." I grabbed Damien by his cheeks and pulled him down to me. "This is the sweetest thing that anyone's ever done for me." My eyes began to burn, but I tried to get them to stop by blinking rapidly.

"Here, have a seat, baby."

He pulled out my chair for me, and I sat down. He pulled the roses off of the table and set them on the counter, and then he pulled two plates out of the oven, sitting one down in front of me. I took a big whiff of the steak, baked potato, and asparagus in front of me.

"This looks amazing. Did you make this yourself?"

I winked at him and smiled. He gave me a smirk before going to the refrigerator and grabbing us both a beer. Damien set my bottle in front of me.

"I did. If you get sick, I'm sorry."

He laughed. I cut into my steak, and as soon as I stuck the piece into my mouth...pure heaven, that's the only way I can describe it. The meat was so tender, it practically melted in my mouth. The baked potato was topped with butter, sour cream, and cheese. The flavor was smooth and creamy on my tongue. I looked up, and Damien was staring at me.

"What? Do I have food on my face?"

He shook his head. "If you don't stop moaning like that, I'm going to throw you over my shoulder, carry you into my bedroom, and fuck you."

My fork froze inches from my mouth, and my mouth hung open. Damien dug into his food, but his eyes were smiling while he chewed on a piece of steak. I shook my head and dug back into my food.

After we finished eating, I cleared the table, but before I could start to clean up, Damien wrapped his arms around my waist. He turned me in his arms and started slow dancing with me.

I smiled up at him. "There's no music playing."

"We don't need it." He twirled me around and around and then pulled me back in, bending down and kissing me thoroughly. "I love you, Carrington."

My body froze, and I looked up at him. I'm such a crybaby, and the tears immediately started leaking from my eyes. "I love you too."

He lifted me up, and I wrapped my legs around his narrow hips as we began to kiss. We didn't stop until we were in his bedroom, and we showed each other just how much we love each other. That was the best night ever.

A smile touches my lips as I think about last Sunday. It was definitely a shift in our relationship.

I don't know how I managed to get so lucky, but one thing still bothers me. He's been so adamant about getting me out of the club, but yet he seems to have no plans to leave. Is it terrible that I really don't want him to still be there? He told me he hasn't slept with any of the dancers, but I don't trust them. Some of the girls have gotten real skanky and whorish. I like sex as much as the next person, but I don't do it for money.

I pull into my parents' driveway. I was surprised when my dad summoned me here via text message. When I step up to the door, my mom greets me with a look on her face that makes me worried.

"What's going on?"

"I don't know. Your dad hasn't told me what's going on, but he's really upset." I follow her inside and down the hall to the family room, where my dad and brother are sitting.

"Hey, guys," I say hesitantly.

"Sit down, Cari." My dad's voice is flat, and he won't even look at me. My stomach rolls as I sit down. My mom sits down next to me. "How's work at the hospital?"

He puts emphasis on the word hospital.

"T-Things a-are g-good, Dad. What's wrong? You're scaring me." I look at my baby brother, and he's looking at me strangely.

My dad grabs his tablet. "Your brother and I were out with your uncles last night, and we're all just playing some pool and your brother and I get a text message. The one I got said," he turns on his tablet. "Oh, here. It says, 'Look at your daughter, aren't you proud? She can work the pole better than anyone can,' and then I get the most entertaining video." I hear "The Hills" by The Weekend start to play, and my stomach turns violently.

"My favorite is the video that was sent to your brother. I really enjoyed watching you give your fucking boyfriend a lap dance in front of your whole audience." Tears start to burn my eyes, but he's not done. He starts to slow clap. "I'm so fucking proud of you, Carrington. You've had us all fooled. Since you were a little girl, you've talked nonstop about becoming a nurse, and when you finally become one, supposedly, you say shit about it. It's all, 'It's good. Learning a lot.' All lies!"

"Daddy."

"No, don't Daddy me. What the fuck?" He's never spoken to me like this before. "Tell me what happened?"

"I didn't pass my boards, and I didn't know what I was going to do because Abby and I already put a deposit down on our apartment. I was driving to the hospital and went past the Thirsty Beaver and decided to stop."

"The Thirsty Beaver? Are you fucking kidding me right now? I can't believe you, Carrington. What the hell? I've heard of that place, and none of it's good. Are you a whore now too?"

A pained cry leaves my lips.

"Dad!" my brother says at the same time my mom says, "Luke."

"I'm embarrassed and disgusted right now, and that boyfriend of yours? He just lets you dance naked in front of a bunch of guys, huh? Doesn't seem like a very good guy to me if he would let you

191

do that."

I'm sobbing now. "Damien's a good p-person. I-I love h-him." My heart is shattering into a million tiny pieces.

My dad barks out a laugh. "You love him? Well, good choice, honey. Maybe you can have him knock you up and then you guys can live off welfare."

I can't listen to this anymore. I'm dying inside, and all I want to do is go home and hide away from the world. Before anyone can stop me, I jump up off of the couch and run through the house until I'm outside, climbing into my car. My brother comes running out after me, but I throw my car in reverse and peel out of the driveway.

Tears run down my face as I drive toward my apartment. My dad and I have always been so close, but the words he said cut me so deep. I pull up to my apartment and run inside, locking the door behind me. My phone is ringing, but I ignore it. I crawl into my bed and cry myself to sleep.

***

I feel my bed move and an arm wrap around my waist. I maneuver myself until I'm facing Abby. "What are you doing here?" My voice is hoarse, and my throat hurts.

"Your mom called mine, and Mom called me. Sweetie, why didn't you tell me what was going on?"

The tears begin to fall again. "We just moved in together, and I knew what a big deal it was for you to be on your own. I didn't want to disappoint you if I couldn't afford it. My dad was so cruel, Abby. He asked me if I was a w-whore."

Just saying it breaks my heart all over again. I close my eyes, wishing this were all a bad dream.

"Oh sweetie, you know he didn't mean it. Your dad loves you."

I push up onto my elbow. "He hates me, Abby. He was so mean to me. I didn't even get to tell them that I finally passed my boards, and as soon as I get my official letter I can apply for a job in the hospital. Tonight's supposed to be my last night dancing at the club."

She hugs me close to her body. I've missed her so much, and I've hated keeping this from her.

"What's it like, dancing topless? Was it scary?" Leave it to her to make me smile.

"It wasn't that scary. I guess it's helped that I've been dancing in front of crowds since I can remember. It was a little weird at first, but then I just pretended that I was dancing for Damien. That helps a lot." I kiss Abby's cheek. "Damien told me he loves me. I love him too."

"Care bear, that's great. I'm so happy for you." Ugh, I hate the nickname that my family gave me when I was really, really little.

"Tell me, how's married life? How's that beautiful little girl?"

Abby's cheeks turn an adorable shade of pink. "It's great! Ben's so amazing. Natalie is so great. I want to have a baby, but Ben wants me to finish school first." That statement causes me to sit up.

"You want to have a baby? Aww…I can't wait

to be an unofficial auntie." I lay back down, and we snuggle like we used to when we were little.

By the time Abby heads home to her family, I feel a bit better, but I'm not sure I can dance tonight. I could just see my dad showing up and causing a scene. A shower sounds good at the moment, so I strip out of my clothes and step into the shower stall. The hot water feels good on my aching muscles and swollen eyes.

While in the shower, I try to calculate in my head the money I have in my checking account, savings account, and what bills I have. I know I'll be fine, but it gives me something to take my mind off of everything.

After I get out of the shower, I use my favorite calming body butter. It's a lavender, chamomile blend. I throw on yoga pants and a sweatshirt and pull my hair up into a ponytail. My phone beeps at me, so I pick it up. I've missed four calls from my mom, five from my brother, and one from my dad.

I delete the voicemails without listening to them. My mom and brother accusing me of being a whore is the last thing that I want to hear right now. They'll show up since I'm not answering, so I need to be gone. Quickly, I throw on my tennis shoes and grab my purse.

Once I'm in my car, I don't know where to go. I don't want to go to Damien. He'd get upset for me, and I don't want him thinking negatively about my dad. I don't want to go to Abby and Ben's. Maybe I'll go to Taylor's. I shoot her a quick text and drive toward her home, but I get a text from Damien asking me to come to the club. I text Taylor and tell

194

her sorry, that I have to go to the club.

It's probably a good thing I'm heading to the club so I can tell them I'm not dancing.

Chapter Nineteen

Damien

My head lulls to the side, and I can barely hold it up. The cobwebs can't seem to clear. Where the fuck am I? I try to move my arms, but they're weighted down. My head tilts forward, and I can see that they're tied to the arm of the chair. As my adrenaline kicks in, the details about how I got here comes back to me.

When I stepped inside, the place was extremely quiet. I moved through the club and back toward Rafe's office. After knocking once, I went inside and found the usual suspects.

"Come in and have a seat, Damien. We've got some things to discuss."

I grabbed a seat next to Bridgette.

"Damien, we had a visitor earlier that might interest you, a Jackson Travis. You remember him. He's the man who attacked Carrington." My hackles had risen because something was not right. I kept my face emotionless. "He brought us a peace offering." Rafe got up from behind his desk and walked around it. He was holding a folder in his hand. "Imagine our surprise when he showed us this." Rafe held a picture in front of me of my ID for the DEA. "We trusted you, and now you're going to pay." A fist connected with my temple, and everything went dark.

I'm fully alert now and see that I'm in one of the private rooms. Tucker comes in a minute later. I jerk in my chair. I'd recognize that red hair anywhere. I'm gagged, but I scream out. Tucker ignores me. He lays Carrington's unconscious body on the sofa and stands in front of me.

"All I had to do was text her from your phone and she delivered herself right to us. We've got lots of fun stuff planned for the two of you, fucking traitor…Pig!"

He punches me right in the face. My head swims, but I breathe through it. I try to talk to him through my gag, and he slips it down.

"Let her go, Tucker. She's not involved in any of this. Don't punish her because of me. Please, she's innocent in all of this. She doesn't even know who I am." He puts the gag back in my mouth.

"We know she is, but we have plans for her while you watch, and it's part of your punishment."

Tucker hangs something from the ceiling and walks back over to Carrington. He slaps her cheek until I watch her jerk awake. I watch helplessly as she realizes something is very wrong.

"Tucker? What's going on?" Her voice sounds tearful.

"Sorry, sweetheart, it's nothing personal." She

fights him as he picks her up like she weighs nothing.

The moment Carrington sees me, she goes ballistic. She slips out of Tucker's grip and runs to me. "Baby, what happened? What did they do to you?" Tucker grabs her and pulls her away from me.

I try to call out to her, but I know she can't understand me. A minute later, Tucker has her arms shackled above her head twenty feet from me. "Please don't do this. Leave us alone." She's crying in earnest now, and I struggle against my restraints.

"Sweet, sweet, Carrington. We're going to have so much fun today. Hang tight."

He laughs as he walks out of the room. The sound of the door locking echoes through the room, and I work the gag partially out of my mouth.

"D-Damien, what's happening? Why are they doing this?" Her arms are stretched high above her, but at least her feet are touching the ground.

"Baby, listen to me, okay? I'm going to try and get us out of here, but I need you to do what I say," I say to her after I work the gag out of my mouth.

"But why are they doing this? What did we do?"

"It's not you, baby. They're doing this because of me. I lied about who I am. I lied to you, and I lied to them." I take a deep breath. My stomach turns. "Baby, I'm with the DEA. I was working here undercover, and that motherfucker, Travis, somehow found out and told them. I'm so fucking sorry."

She doesn't say anything. Her cries say it all. I want nothing more than to hold her, but I can't

198

fucking move.

I'm not sure how much time passes, but I hear the lock disengage, and the door swings open. Rafe, Bridgette, and Tucker come walking in. I take a blow to the face from both Rafe and Tucker, but I don't feel it because I'm watching Bridgette walk slowly around Carrington.

"P-Please l-let me go. I-I didn't do anything. Bridgette, please." My girl sounds so broken right now, it's killing me.

"Sweet, little Carrington. We can't do that, and Damien…or, I'm sorry, David needs to pay for what he's done, and unfortunately for you, you're part of his payment."

I struggle against my bindings as Bridgette pulls out a large knife. Carrington cries as Bridgette cuts her sweatshirt and yoga pants off, leaving my girl in her bra and panties. "Oh baby, you have such a beautiful body." Bridgette drags her hand over Carrington's stomach and then up to her bra-covered breasts.

"Stop touching her, bitch!" I yell. I feel a hand grip my hair, wrenching my head back. A fist hits my stomach, causing me to wheeze and gag.

Rafe gets in my face. "You shut the fuck up. This is all on you. You tried to weasel your way into our operation so you could gather information to have us shut down. I trusted you." He punches me in the stomach and then in the face.

"Please stop hitting him!" Carrington pleads.

"Oh, she wants me to stop hitting you, Damien. Maybe I'll just go over there to Carrington."

I jerk harder against my bindings while Rafe

199

moves to stand right behind Carrington. He winds his arm around her and palms her breasts. Carrington tries to fight him off, but he's too strong.

"I've been dying to get my hands on you." Rafe bites her earlobe, and I want to fucking kill him for touching her.

Tucker's arms are wrapped around Bridgette, and he's kissing on her neck. My eyes move back to Rafe and Carrington. Rafe gives me a smile that makes my stomach turn. Rafe hits Carrington with his elbow right in the stomach. Carrington cries out and gasps for air.

"Motherfucker!"

I throw my chair to the side try to break it, my eyes never leaving Carrington as Rafe grabs her hair and pulls her head back. She coughs and spits while still gasping for air. Bridgette leans forward, dragging her tongue up Carrington's neck.

"I'm sorry," I mouth to her as I watch the tears slide down her cheeks.

The three of them aren't paying attention to me. I wiggle a little in my seat and feel one of my bindings loosen a little. "Get the fuck off of her." Tucker and Rafe come over and pull me up off of the floor. "If you're going to kill me, just fucking do it already. Let her go." I hold perfectly still so they can't see that my left hand can move a bit.

***

At least four hours have gone by since this ordeal started. I was hoping they'd have to move us due to the club opening, but apparently they've shut the bar down for tonight, just for us. I've loosened the rope a bit more, but my arm is sore as fuck. Carrington's arms are still above her head. Her cries come and go, and they ignored her pleas to use the bathroom so she ended up going right there on the floor. The look of humiliation on her face recharged my motivation to try and get the rope loose.

"Baby? How are you doing, Carrington? I'm going to get us out of here."

Her head is hanging forward, and she's not really responding to me. I'm not sure if it's because she's mad at me or because she's zoned out. I honestly hope she's zoned out. It'll help her deal with everything for the time being.

"I want to go home." Her voice is so quiet that I can barely hear her. "Please just let me go home. I don't want to die."

Her words break my heart. I start working on the rope again, this time a lot harder. The sound of me sawing on the rope with a tiny piece of metal sticking out of the chair echoes in the room loudly, or at least to me it sounds loud.

I feel it give a bit more. If I could, I'd give a happy shout, but I don't. The door opens and Bridgette walks in; grabbing a chair so it's in front of me, she sits down, crossing one leg over the other. We stare at each other, neither looking away. I have no clue why they sent her.

"You know, David. You're a very good actor. We were all fooled. I've always prided myself on the ability to read people, but you fooled me. When I brought Rafe and Tucker on, I knew they were special, and I was right. They'd been running and dealing for two years and never got caught. When I decided to expand the business, they were wonderful assets."

She's the boss. Sonofabitch. They were good about keeping it a secret, that's for sure.

I'm not saying shit to her. I want her gone so I can work on the rope some more. Bridgette looks behind her at Carrington and then back at me.

"What do you think we should do with her? I'd like to take her home and keep her. Rafe said that he'd love to keep her. Who do you think she'd like to be with more?"

She stands up and moves behind her chair and leans forward, kissing Carrington's cheek. "I'll be back."

As soon as she's gone, I start furiously working on the rope. I feel the exact moment that the rope gives way enough for me to slide my hand out. With quick movements, I get the other rope undone and then work on my legs. My body protests when I stand up, but I ignore it. When I reach Carrington, I undo the restraints around her wrists.

"Baby, I'm going to help you put your arms down. I'm not going to lie, it's going to hurt, but try not to make any noise."

"O-Okay." As I lower her arms, she bites her lip as she moans. She sounds like a wounded animal. I try to rub her shoulders and arms for her to help get the blood flow going.

"I'm fine," she tells me.

As I move toward the door, I don't hear anything. The idiots have phones in the rooms, so I make my way toward it and dial 9-1-1. I give them my badge number and the information I have.

I slip my jacket onto Carrington since she's just wearing a bra and panties and her panties are wet.

"We're going to try and sneak out the back, okay?" I whisper. She nods her head and then reaches up, touching my eye that I can't see out of. I kiss her hand, and tell her, "I'm okay." I slide my hands into her hair and kiss her lips. "I'm going to make this right."

With her hand in mine, Carrington and I move toward the door. I test the door, and it's locked.

"Okay, baby. This is what we're going to do."

I tell her my plan and hopefully, by the time shit goes down, backup will here.

Chapter Twenty

Carrington

Damien, or David, hands me a leg of one of the metal chairs and moves me so I'll be behind the door when it opens. He grabs his own chair, and then we wait. My whole body trembles as I hold my makeshift weapon and wait for the signal to go. I just want to go home and shower all of the yuck off of me. I feel disgusting. Just the thought of any of them touching me again makes my stomach turn violently.

My thoughts are all over the place while we wait for someone to come back. Once this is over, I just want to move on and forget this chapter of my life ever happened. My relationship is ruined with my dad. Damien lied to me about everything, and I knew something was wrong with Bridgette. I just wasn't expecting her to be the big boss of everything.

With my forehead resting against the wall, I take some deep breaths. I can feel Damien's eyes on me, but I don't look. I can't. I'm so hurt and tired, and I'm mentally done. I have just enough fight in me to help get us out of here.

I hear a noise in the hall. Damien nods at me, and I hold my chair leg up, ready to swing it.

The lock disengages, and the door slowly opens. Tucker steps into the room, and I watch as Damien swings his chair at him, taking him down with one shot. Damien grabs my hand, and we move quickly. We run out into the hall, heading in the direction of the back door. I hear the unmistakable click of a gun behind us. We both turn to find Bridgette and Rafe standing there. Rafe looks really mad.

"You better hope that Tucker wakes up," he growls at us.

Damien moves so he's in front of me. My body is trembling so bad that my teeth are chattering. I move closer to his back, burying my face in his shirt, trying to take comfort in the warmth of his skin and his familiar scent.

"He'll wake up. He just took a blow to the head, but not hard enough to kill," Damien says. We keep inching backward toward the door. All I want to do right now is make a run for it, but that'll just get me shot. "Why don't we let Carrington go, and you can do whatever you want to me."

"Oh, we're going to do whatever we want with you whether she's here or not. Better yet, Carrington, come here." Neither of us moves. "Maybe if I put a bullet in him, you'll move."

My body tenses. I don't want Damien getting hurt because of me. I step around him, but Damien wraps his arm around my waist and pulls me toward

205

his chest. "Let her go, Pig."

Rafe fires the gun, aiming at the floor by Damien's feet.

I scream and jump. Tucker comes stumbling out of the room and lunges for Damien. He knocks into me, and I go flying backward as Tucker and Damien hit the floor. Bridgette stalks over and, with a firm grip in my hair, pulls me up off of the floor and drags me with her over to Rafe. She thrusts me toward Rafe.

"Get her out of here." Rafe grabs me in a punishing grip and starts dragging me toward the front of the club. I fight him with everything I have.

We're almost halfway through the club when chaos ensues. The club is immediately filled with smoke, and there's a lot of shouting. I get down on the floor, covering my head, trying to cover up my coughing. I'm not sure how much time passes before the smoke clears.

It sounds like it's far away when I hear someone yell, "She's in here."

I don't dare look, and I try to make myself as small as possible. A hand touches my back, and a frightened scream leaves my mouth. "Miss, you're okay. I'm an agent, and I'm here just to get you outside and to the waiting ambulance. I'm going to pick you up, okay?"

I nod my head. As he moves to scoop me up, I whisper, "I-I a-accidentally w-wet myself."

He gives me a warm smile and nods before lifting me like I weigh nothing. I wrap my arms around his shoulders and bury my face in his neck as the tears start to fall in earnest.

The cool air hits me as we step outside. I start trembling so bad that my body starts hurting. The man carrying me picks up speed, and then I'm lifted out of his arms and laid on a gurney.

"Miss, we're going to try and warm you up. You're shivering pretty bad right now."

The man lays a couple of warm blankets on me. I curl in on myself as the EMT checks my vitals. He talks to his partner, but I don't listen. I just close my eyes and imagine I'm somewhere else.

I hear another voice and recognize it's Damien, or David…whatever he really goes by.

"Agent Michaels, we're taking her in to get checked out. They've recommended you get your face checked out."

"I'm riding in here then," Damien says.

"Sir, that's against policy."

"I don't give a shit. I'm not moving."

I hear more grumbling and then hear the doors shut. Damien rubs my back as the ambulance starts moving. My eyes start to feel heavy, so I welcome sleep.

***

I've been poked and prodded since they wheeled me in to the emergency room. At first they wouldn't let Damien stay with me, but that was the only way that he'd agree to let anyone check him out. I ignored everyone and only spoke to the nurse when she was in the room and then the doctor when he came to look me over and tell me that he was ordering x-rays of my shoulders since they'd been stretched for so long. An agent came and got Damien a while ago, so I've been alone.

"I want to see my daughter and I want to see her now."

I hear my dad's voice from the hall just before the curtain is moved and he walks in, followed by my mom. I roll over so I'm facing the opposite way. I don't really want to hear, *I told you so*, right now.

"Oh, my sweet girl. Are you okay?" My mom is right in front of me, stroking my hair. A tear leaks from my eye, but she quickly wipes it away. "No tears, baby. You're safe. We talked to Damien and he told us what he does. I'm not real thrilled that he lied to my baby, but he's a good man who is very worried about you right now."

A hand on my leg causes me to jerk it away. I look and see that the hand belonged to my dad. Lying back down, I shut my eyes and wish they would just leave. The doctor comes in a few minutes later.

"Carrington, how are you feeling?"

"Cold, tired, and sore. My stomach's been cramping a little." The doctor looks at my chart and then back up at me.

"Did you know that you're pregnant?"

My ears starting ringing. "What? No."

"I'm going to order an ultrasound, but the cramping has me worried. Now, you said that you were hit in the stomach hard. Is that correct?"

Tears fill my eyes, and my mom grabs my hands in both of hers. She pulls them to her mouth and kisses them. "Um, yes. O-One of the m-men hit me with his elbow, really hard." My dad growls and curses under his breath.

"Okay, we'll get that ultrasound ordered right away. We'll try to get them in here as soon as possible."

As soon as the doctor's gone, I look at my dad, expecting to see disapproval on his face, but instead I see a look of sadness and uncertainty. My mom sits on the side of my bed and bends down, kissing my head. "It's going to be okay, my beautiful girl."

Since Damien left earlier, he hasn't been back. I guess now that his case is done, he's done with me.

The tech and the doctor come into the room, and I ask my mom to stay. My dad kisses my forehead and excuses himself. They put my legs in stirrups, put a condom on the wand, and then put some of jelly on the end of it. "Okay, Carrington. You're going to feel a little bit of pressure."

I feel the wand enter me and then the pressure he said to expect. "Okay, here we go." He moves the screen so I can see it. "Here's the heartbeat. From your last period and the measurements, I would estimate you're about five weeks along." He moves the want a bit. "What do we have here? There's another sack, but I'm sorry to say there's no heartbeat."

He asks my mom about twins, but all I can hear is *no heartbeat*. I see the doctor's lips moving and my mom's moving as she nods her head. The doctor pulls out the wand and helps me sit up.

"Carrington, I want you to follow up with an OB/GYN this week. Your body will absorb the other sack or the other baby will. It's completely natural for this to happen, and since there were two separate sacks there should be no risk of miscarrying, but that's why I want you to follow up this week. They're going to get your discharge papers together, and we'll get you out of here."

It takes an hour before I'm finally released. The aide comes in with a wheelchair, and she helps me up and into the chair. She starts pushing me down the hall with my mom following closely behind. I wasn't sure where my dad went until we make it out front and he's standing by the doors, staring blindly out the window.

He sees us and comes over to tell Mom that he's going to get the car. Great, he can't even speak to me. I'm sure he's now even more disappointed in his knocked up, former stripper daughter.

After loading me in the car, they head toward town. It doesn't even dawn on me that they drive right by my apartment. When we reach my parents' home, I climb out of the backseat. My mom wraps her arm around my waist and we follow my dad inside.

"Sweetheart, your brother changed the sheets in your old room. Go lay down and I'll bring you some soup in a little bit."

***

Damien

It's been a week since everything went down, and things have been crazy. We've interrogated Rafe, Tucker, and Bridgette multiple times, but we haven't gotten very far. The plan is to try and get them to flip on each other. My boss, Hector, wanted me to take some time off, but I'm doing everything in my power to make sure these three pieces of shit stay behind bars. One good thing is that piece of shit Jackson Travis is locked up and won't be out for a long time.

I've had to fill out so much paperwork and write so many reports, I'm over it. I've been camped out in a hotel in Charleston this past week since this is the office I'm working out of. I've tried calling Carrington multiple times, but I haven't been able to reach her. I did get a hold of her mom, and she assured me that Carrington was okay, but I felt like there was something I was missing.

My hope is to be done here in the next few days, get down to Beaufort, and talk to her to see where her head is at. I hated just leaving her, but I knew her parents would be there, and I wanted to start working right away to make sure the evil trio stays where they are.

Fuck, if I'm being honest, part of the reason is because of guilt. It was my fault that she even went through everything that she did. I didn't protect her the way I should've. I never should have gotten involved with her, but I did and I fell in love with her.

I had to let my parents know what happened and assure them that I was okay after my mom stopped crying. It was time to tell them everything about Carrington. My mom asked lots of questions about her, and when the time is right, she wants to meet her.

I really need to see her, so I hop into my Jeep

and head to her parents' place. I try to play out different scenarios in my head, but I might just be better off winging it.

An hour later, I pull in front of Carrington's parents' house because I know that's where she's staying. I climb out and make my way toward their front door. Her mom opens it before I even have a chance to knock. She looks extremely surprised that I'm here.

"Damien?"

"Hi, Mrs. Carter. I was hoping I could see Carrington."

She opens the door for me, and I step inside.

"That's good. Maybe you can convince her to leave her room. I've gotten her out once for a doctor's appointment, but other than that she won't leave. She's in the second room on the left."

My eyes go to the pictures on the wall, and a smile graces my lips as I look at pictures of Carrington from baby to teen. There is one that catches my attention. It's her parents and her as a tiny baby. You can just see the love that they have for her. It's a black and white photo. Her dad is lying on his back, Carrington is on his chest, and her mom is lying on her side with a hand on Carrington's little baby diapered butt. They're looking at her like she's the greatest treasure in the world, because she fucking is.

I move down the hall, giving a little knock before opening the door. My girl is asleep in her bed. I toe off my shoes and slide into bed with her. I pull her into my arms, and everything feels right with the world. I sift my hand through her hair.

While I hold her, I close my eyes and pray that she forgives me for everything.

I don't fall asleep, but I slip into a relaxed state and it feels fantastic. Carrington stirs next to me, and I kiss her forehead.

"Damien?"

"Yeah, baby, I'm here."

With quick movements, Carrington lunges for the side of the bed, throwing up into the garbage can. I rub her back as she pukes over and over. When she finally stops I help her back up on the bed. I get a closer look at her. She looks exhausted, pale, and there arc shadows under her eyes.

"Are you okay?"

"Yeah, it's just morning sickness."

I freeze, and she must realize what she said because she looks at me with wide eyes.

"A-Are you pregnant?" She nods her head. I pull her into a hug. Wow. Um—a baby. "Wow, I'm kind of in shock right now. When did you find out?"

"At the hospital, after everything happened. There were two babies, but there was no heartbeat on one when they did the ultrasound. The doctor said there was still a heartbeat on the baby that was left." She grabs a can of ginger ale off of her nightstand and takes a sip. "I'm so sorry, Damien."

"You've got nothing to be sorry about. Baby, you weren't alone. I'm the one who's sorry. We'll figure it out, okay? I love you."

"Why haven't I seen you until now? You just left me at the hospital. I needed you, and you weren't there. I had to hear that one of our babies didn't make it, alone. Let's talk about the fact that you're not who you say you are. Was everything a lie? Do you truly even love me, or was I just part of your job?"

She's letting me have it, but it's what I totally deserve.

"Baby, I wanted to tell you so many times, but I couldn't. I couldn't risk your safety, but fuck, I couldn't keep you safe anyway. I will never forgive myself for what happened. You haven't seen me because I've been working round the clock to make sure they stay locked up. We've arrested Jackson, not only for attacking you, but he's the one who figured out who I am and told Rafe about it. He's looking at serious jail time." I reach out and stroke her cheek.

There's a knock on the door, and we both turn toward it. Her mom is at the door. "Dinner's ready. Care bear, do you think you can get some food down?"

"Yeah, I think so."

"Okay, good. Damien, are you staying?" she asks.

"That'd be great, thanks." I get off Carrington's bed and help her up. She lets me pull her toward me and hug her close. "Is it okay if I stay?" I won't stay if Carrington doesn't want me to.

"Of course you can stay."

I wrap my arm around her shoulders as we head out into the dining room. Her dad and brother are sitting at the table. Something is going on with her and her dad. She won't look at him, and he looks like he wants to go to her. Her brother, Luke, gets up and comes around the table to hug her.

"You look like shit," he says to her.

She slaps at his chest and gives him a smile. Luke's right, though. She looks green. I've been around pregnant women before and I know this is normal, especially the first few months.

I shake her dad's hand. He doesn't punch me, so I'm going to guess that he doesn't completely hate me for getting his daughter pregnant. He is staring at me, though. Maybe he's merely plotting my death and he's choosing to have me live in fear. I'm a big guy and even taller than him, but I'm intimidated as hell right now. I want to know what's going on with him and Carrington.

Chicken sandwiches are passed around, and then what looks like homemade macaroni and cheese. Carrington sets a bowl of salad in front of each of us. I scoop a huge bite of the macaroni and cheese into my mouth. It's amazing, and I try not to moan and embarrass myself.

"This is amazing, Mrs. Carter."

"Damien, please call me Bellamy."

Carrington sits next to me and pushes her food around on her plate. I feel bad because it's technically my fault she's suffering right now. Reaching out, I rub my hand up and down her back.

"Are you okay, baby? Do you want your ginger ale?"

"My stomach's turning a little bit."

"I'll be right back." I run back to her room and grab the open can off of her nightstand. I set it down in front of her and take my seat.

After dinner, Carrington and I sit on the back deck. "Baby, what happened with your dad? I can tell that things are strained between you."

She spends the next ten minutes telling me about her dad and brother getting text messages and videos, outing her as a stripper. Her dad didn't take it well. I don't really like the fact that he asked her if she was a whore. By the time she's done telling me everything, she's crying against my chest. I hold her close, rubbing her back as she lets it all out. It's obvious Carrington loves her dad a lot, and his disapproval really hurts her.

My baby falls asleep against my chest. I pick her up and carry her into the house. Her mom gives me a smile as I pass by. I lay her down on her mattress and cover her with her blankets. She immediately snuggles in, so I place the trashcan by the side of the bed just in case.

I kiss her forehead and then back out of her room quietly. In the living room, I find her dad sitting on the sofa.

"Do you have a minute to talk, sir?" He nods and stands up.

"Let's go outside." I follow behind him as he steps out onto the front porch.

"Jackson Travis is behind bars. It was he who found out who I was and turned me in. They picked him up last week, and he won't be getting out for a while. The people I was investigating are behind bars as well. I doubt they'll get out anytime soon." He nods his head at me. "Sir, I didn't mean for her to get hurt. I tried to stay away from her, but she's got this light about her that draws me in."

When the hell did I get so mushy? Her dad probably thinks I'm a pussy.

Chapter Twenty-One

Luke

I'll admit when I first heard that Damien was an undercover agent, it gave me bad flashbacks of another DEA agent that started out good and then turned into a nightmare, almost ruining our family's lives.

"Damien, no one blames you for anything that happened. I blame that piece of shit, Jackson. Hope for a boy because having a girl ages you very quickly. I'm just kidding, sort of. The first time I held her, I was scared to death. She was just so tiny and perfect. I'd never believed in love at first sight until I saw that little angel. There were many times that she would look up at me with those big blue eyes and I would do anything for her, give her anything she wanted." I take a deep breath. "I've made so many mistakes when it comes to my girl.

That whole situation with that fucking teacher hurt our relationship. I blamed her, but it wasn't her fault. She's always been beautiful, and I guess I just hated the idea of any man paying her any attention."

"I can imagine. I suppose I'd probably be the same way if this baby is a girl. I plan to marry her, just so you know. I want her and our baby to have my last name." Damien looks sincere.

"I'm going to be a grandpa," I whisper. "Wow!"

I want to be upset that my baby girl is having a baby, but I'm just happy.

"It kills me that she's not speaking to me. I know I fucked up when I found out about her dancing, but just the thought of perverts watching my little girl dance became too much. The things I said to her...Jesus, I was cruel. I just don't know how to fix it."

"Daddy?" I turn around and find my daughter in the doorway.

She steps outside and moves until she's right in front of me. Damien excuses himself and disappears inside the house.

"You are the light of my life. You and your brother are the best things that ever happened to me. I'm sorry what I said hurt you."

"I've always felt like I was never good enough for you. I've always felt like I was just a replacement child for Rose."

I'm floored that she'd felt that way. Yes, Bellamy and I still mourn the child we lost, but that was not the reason why we had kids.

"Baby, no. Fuck, no. You were never a replacement for Rose. I'm sorry if you ever thought that. I'm sorry that you felt like you weren't good enough. We love you so much and are so proud of you. You've got such a big heart, and the way you care for others is why I know you're going to be an amazing nurse and you're going to be a phenomenal mother."

Carrington wraps her arms around my waist. I hug her tight and feel the burning behind my eyelids start, but I try to blink the tears back. I look up and find my wife standing in the doorway watching us with tears rolling down her cheeks. She wraps her arms around us.

Our girl finally stops crying, and I kiss the top of her head before I watch her disappear inside, presumably to find Damien. I look down at my wife, who still has her arms around me. Twenty-two years of marriage and this woman still knows how to make my heart skip a beat.

***

Bellamy

Hearing my daughter say that she'd always felt like a replacement for her sister rips me apart. I try to think back to the past and if I ever gave her any indication that she was a replacement, and I can't think of anything. Of course, there isn't a day that I don't think about our beautiful Rose. She'd be twenty-eight if she were alive, but with time I finally accepted that she was meant to be my angel. Carrington has been such a blessing, and I hate the fact that we ever made her feel like she wasn't.

When they laid her on my chest the day she was born, she opened her eyes and looked up at me and I felt peace. She was perfect in every way.

When I step outside, I wrap my arms around my beautiful husband and my gorgeous daughter. Carrington excuses herself and goes back in the house.

Damien leaves a short time later, and I make my way down the hall to Carrington's old room. I find her lying against a stack of pillows. "Hey, baby girl. How are you feeling?"

"Good. Tired. Damien went to get me some ice cream. Is that okay, that he comes back?" Carrington stifles a yawn with the back of her hand.

"Of course. Don't worry. In a couple of months, you'll feel better. The beginning is always the toughest. Honey, I just wanted to say that I'm sorry if I ever made you feel like you were a replacement for Rose or that you were somehow second best." Tears start to cloud my vision, and I try to swipe them quickly away. "You and your brother are the best things to every happen to your dad and me." I feel Carrington's arms wrap around me as we both begin to cry.

My girl and I lie side by side while she asks me about being pregnant and what to expect. When Damien comes back in the room with a pint of ice cream and a spoon, I take my leave, but not before I kiss my daughter on the forehead and kiss Damien on the cheek.

As I shut the door behind me, I see Damien situate Carrington so she's sitting up and then feeds her the ice cream. He's looking at her the same way

Luke has always looked at me. I head out into the kitchen, smiling. I know my girl is going to be just fine.

***

Carrington

It's been a month since everything went down. Things have slowly been getting better. I got my letter that says I passed my boards, so I'm officially an RN. I'm now in orientation in the ER, where I'll be working three twelve-hour shifts. I'll have full benefits, and as soon as the baby's born, my baby will have coverage too.

I'm not getting nearly as sick as I did a month ago, but my doctor doesn't like that I haven't gained any weight, so I've been chugging down protein shakes, which has helped. Damien and I are dividing our time between my place and his. We've started talking about whether we want to just have him move him into my place for the time being or find something completely different.

Speaking of my man, I see his Jeep pull into the parking lot. He's coming with me to my OB appointment today, and we're hoping to maybe hear the heartbeat. I climb out of my car and tie my coat around me just a little bit tighter. Ugh, he's so sexy. His jeans hug his thighs and showcase his beautiful dick, making my mouth water.

We haven't had sex since before our ordeal. Of course, most of the reason we haven't is because I was getting sick all of the time. God, I'm so fucking horny right now.

"Babe, don't look at me like that. Otherwise we're going to have to find a bathroom or dark hallway to fuck in." He bends down and kisses my lips. "Did you get sick this morning?"

"No, I actually felt a little bit better today. Can you meet me at home after our appointment?" I walk my fingers up his hard chest. If he stuck his hand in my panties, he'd find me wet.

Hand in hand, we walk inside. I check in at the desk and then sit with him while we wait for my name to be called. Once I get called back, we go through the normal stuff: weight, blood pressure, and temperature. As soon as the nurse leaves the room Damien steps between my legs and kisses my lips thoroughly. I asked if I should call him David, but he said he likes me calling him Damien.

The doctor comes in a few minutes later, and I introduce them. She asks me about getting sick and about my energy level. I lie back on the table while she feels around. Then she grabs the Doppler and the jelly. "Okay, guys, let's see if we can hear your baby's heart beat."

Damien grabs hold of my hand as the doctor squirts some of the jelly onto my still flat stomach. There's a lot of static and then the most beautiful sound in the world. Tears run down my face in response to the rapid beating of our baby's heart.

Damien pulls my hand to his lips and kisses them. "That's the most beautiful sound I've ever heard." His voice sounds like it's thick with unshed tears.

She tells us everything sounds good and looks

good. For the time being, she wants me to continue drinking those shakes and says she'll see me in a month. On our way out, I schedule my appointment and then we head to the parking lot.

"I'll meet you at your place," he says before disappearing.

"Finally," I mutter to myself.

***

While I'm on my hands and knees, Damien slowly eases in and out of me. I'm so close to coming again it's not even funny. When we got home, first he ate my pussy while I was spread out on the sofa in the living room and then he carried me to my bed and made me come again just by sucking on my tits, which are highly sensitive at the moment. He put me in the position that I am right now in lightning speed.

It's been too long, and I feel like I'm stuffed so full. I've missed this, missed the feel of him inside me. He kisses my back as he continues to move so slowly in and out of me.

"I've missed your pussy. You feel so good. You're squeezing my dick so good, baby," he whispers against my skin. I whimper when he reaches around and rubs clit, working me up to an orgasm that threatens to annihilate me. His strokes are short, each hitting my sweat spot. My cries fill the room, and I feel an orgasm coming.

"Oh yeah, baby. I can feel it coming. Rub your clit for me." He grabs my hips, and as I rub my clit, he pounds into me with punishing strokes.

223

I fuck myself on his cock and squeeze my clit between my fingers as I hurtle toward my orgasm. He thrusts once, twice, and I come so hard, my head flies back. Damien plants himself deep, and I feel the hot blast of his come over and over. He places his lips against my neck and squeezes me tightly. With another kiss, he pulls out of me and collapses next to me.

"Come here, baby." He pulls me toward him until we're chest to chest. With a tender touch, he brushes my hair out of my face. "I fucking love you."

He reaches down, covering my lower belly, where our baby rests.

"I love you too," I whisper.

In the dark of my room, snuggled together, Damien and I make plans for our future—a future that is going to be amazing. Together we can do anything.

Epilogue

Carrington

Three Years Later

"Bed two is waiting for a room upstairs. I checked her IV bag, and it's about halfway done. Bed four is waiting for CT, but they're backed up. Other than that, it's all good," I tell my relief, Jessica. It was a long shift today, and I just want to get home and off of my feet.

"Thanks, Cari. See you Friday," Jessica says as I wave goodbye and head to the locker room. I've been working here at Lutheran Hospital as an ER nurse for the past two and a half years, and I love it. Emergency medicine was definitely the right choice for me. It's fast paced and challenging. Coincidentally, I work with Abby's mother in law, who's a nurse practitioner, and she's phenomenal. I've learned so much from Jackie.

It's hot out today as I change into my tank top maxi dress, one that Taylor bought for me, and flip-flops. I turn on my phone and send a quick text to Damien's mom, Carol, to let her know that I'm on my way. The first time I met her and Damien's dad, Roger, I was nervous and scared, but I immediately fell in love with both of them. Victoria, Damien's baby sister, and I have gotten very close over the past couple of years as well.

As I make my way toward Carol and Roger's place, I can't help but think about the past few years. Shortly after my twelfth week of pregnancy, I ended up having a miscarriage. Damien and I both struggled with our grief, but luckily my parents were there as a huge support system for us. Yes, the circumstances were different, but it still wasn't any less painful. We both wanted our baby but knew it was just nature's way of telling us that something wasn't right. As time went on, the grief was less and less. Oh, it was still there, but it wasn't nearly as overwhelming.

Six months later, I became pregnant again. We weren't trying, but I swear he has super sperm, and surprise, surprise I was pregnant with twins. So, almost two years ago, I gave birth to my sweet baby girl and boy, Shay and Ryder. Having one of each was perfect, and they're the best kids a girl could ask for. They love each other so much and often entertain each other.

They keep us on our toes, but I wouldn't have it any other way. After pulling in to the driveway, I get out and make my way toward the front door. I knock and head inside.

"Hello!" I call out.

"Hey, honey, we're back here." I step down the

hall and find Carol and Victoria sitting on the floor with the kids.

"Hi, guys. Hi, my beautiful babies."

Shay gets up and gives me a big smile. I scoop her up in my arms and listen as she tells me a story in her baby talk and then points at her brother. "Oh yeah. Tell Mommy all about it." Ryder comes over to me, and I put Shay down and pick up my boy. "Hi, handsome. Did you miss Mommy?" He grabs my cheeks and pulls me toward him for a wet, slobbery kiss.

Carol tells me about their day and how the kids behaved. Between her and my mom, we haven't had to pay for day care. They usually alternate weeks. That way, one doesn't get more time than the other.

"Sweetheart, how are you feeling?"

"Good, tired. This little one is sucking the life out of me, and we double-checked. There's only one this time."

If Damien doesn't go get a vasectomy after this baby is born, I'm going to do it myself because three children under three years of age is going to keep us very busy.

We visit for a little longer, and then they help me load the kids into my minivan. I hug and kiss both women and make my way home.

We bought our home about three months before the twins came, which was crazy, but our families all helped us get it ready. We live between his parents' house and mine in a cute little three-bedroom ranch. It has a huge porch that I love to sit in when it's nice out.

I pull into the driveway and find my man

working on his motorcycle. He looks up and gives me that smile that can still make my panties wet and moves toward the other side of the van to get Ryder out.

We meet at the front, and he bends down to kiss me. "How was your day, babe?"

"Good, busy. I could really use a soak in the tub."

"Let me finish out here and I'll be in shortly so you can do that." He kisses me one more time and then helps me get the kids inside before heading back out.

Bathing both kids is a feat, but it's easier to do both at once than one at a time. They love their bath time, and I swear more soapy water gets on me and the floor than them, but I honestly don't care. I just love watching them squeal and splash. After pulling the little prunes out, I get them dried off, lotioned up, diapered, and dressed.

They're both having their bedtime bottles when Damien comes in. He sits next to us on the sofa and pulls Ryder onto his lap, kissing his dark brown locks. They both have Damien's dark hair, but Shay has a hint of red in hers. They both have my blue eyes and my dimples. I can't wait to see who the next one looks like.

After the twins go down for the night, I run my bath, and while the tub fills up I look at myself in the mirror. I'm only four months along, but I'm already showing, which they said would happen. I've kept in pretty good shape, but my breasts aren't as perky as they were and my nipples are huge. I did breastfeed two babies for almost a year, so I shouldn't be surprised.

The door opens, and I find my husband staring at me. "You look so fucking gorgeous." He moves toward me and bends down, kissing my lips. "How about company in the bath."

Damien strips out of his clothes and then helps me into the tub. Once we're settled in, I have a feeling it's going to be a while before I actually get clean.

***

Damien

Five Years Later

I flip the burgers and hot dogs on the grill when my father-in-law, Luke, stands next to me. We had a rocky relationship in the beginning, but after Cari and I lost our baby, things shifted between us. He's become a great friend and someone I always feel like I can talk to.

"Everything looks great. The kids seem to be having a blast."

We rented a house on the beach with her parents and mine. Everyone's been having fun. I look toward the water, where my beautiful wife is dancing around with our daughters, Shay and Kara, dancing behind her. Ryder's not too far from his mom and sisters, but he's playing with our boxer, Chief.

I continued to work for the DEA until right after Kara was born. It was a decision that I didn't make lightly, but I needed something with a little more stability. I became a detective with the Beaufort PD four years ago and couldn't be happier.

"Yeah, they are. I think this is going to become an annual thing. I hope you're okay with that."

"Absolutely. Bellamy loves any chance she gets to be with the kids." He places a hand on my shoulder, getting my full attention. "You two are amazing parents. I just want you to know that I think you're doing a fantastic job with those kids. They're loving, funny, but they listen and behave and have manners. Not a lot of kids are like that these days."

"You can thank your daughter for that. She's been very big on the kids always saying please and thank you for everything."

"Well, it doesn't matter, because you guys are a team. I know I've said it before, but I couldn't be more proud of the man my daughter ended up with."

I don't even know what to say after that. I just give him a chin lift.

***

The sound of the surf comes through the window as I lie in bed with Carrington in my arms. With a houseful, I've had to get real creative about fucking my wife. Tonight it was in the inside of our closet with my hand over her mouth. She came so hard that she squeezed my come right out of me.

Her soft breathing tickles my chest. I let my fingers drift up and down her body and smile as I watch goose bumps pop up all over her body. I never in my life imagined my life would be so full, but dammit it is. Those babies of mine have turned me in to a sentimental asshole, but really, who cares? I'm happy, she's happy, and our kids are happy. That's all that matters to me.

Forbidden Love

Book 3 in the Love Stings Series

Chapter One

Violet

The apartment that my parents are helping me rent looms in front of me, and a sense of excitement runs through me. Last year I stayed in the dorms, and it wasn't bad. It just wasn't good either. My roommate was a party girl, and I was not. My dad just about had a nervous breakdown when he found out I was moving into coed dorms.

My dad is a little on the overprotective side. Okay, little is putting it mildly. My dad would keep me and my sisters locked away if he could. I'm okay with it. I'm a total daddy's girl. He and I have always had a special bond. I'm even going to Tulane to major in architecture and minor in business. My hope is to work alongside my dad and uncles. They run the construction and restoration company that my grandpa and his best friend started a long time ago.

When I was little, I used to go to work with my dad when I could and I soaked up all of the knowledge I got from watching him work. It was a natural next step to go to my dad's alma mater.

My mom and I climb out of my car, and my dad and uncle climb out of the moving truck.

"I don't like it. That's it, we're moving you home," my dad says from behind me.

"Daddy, you don't mean that. This is a safe building. You have to buzz to get in."

When I first approached my parents about living off campus, my mom was all for it, but my dad took a little convincing. He only agreed when I let him help me search. We found the perfect spot. I'm five minutes from campus and close to the campus library, where I work. It's a one-bedroom apartment with a tiny eat-in kitchen and a cute little deck that I'll be able to sit out on.

We all work together to get my stuff unloaded. My mom and I found the cutest used furniture at a flea market that gives my place a kitschy look, which is just my style. My dad calls me his little gypsy, but I call it bohemian. My dark hair hangs down to my lower back in wild waves, and I wear a lot of maxi skirts or dresses with bangles on my wrists and ears full of earrings.

Once the last box is brought in, my dad and uncle go to get us pizza. I sit on my love seat with my mom. "I love this place, Mom. Thank you for all of your help." She kisses my forehead.

"You bet, baby. I hope you have such a good time, but not too good," she says with a goofy smile on her face.

"Please, I'll be too busy studying to have any fun at all. I have Mr. Torres for studio work in architectural design. I guess he's really tough and kind of an asshole, but I can handle him. I hope."

Playlist for Secret Love

You and I–Lady Gaga
Cool for the Summer–Demi Lovato
F**k Around (All Night)–Pepper
I'm on Fire–Slightly Stoopid
Down Down Down–The Expendables
Stroke Me–Mickey Avalon
Sirens (Feat. Dirty Heads)–Sublime with Rome
The Hills–The Weeknd
Problem–Natalia Kills
Here–Alessia Cara
Revolution–Diplo
Everywhere I Go–Hollywood Undead
Come Around–Slightly Stoopid
Boombastic–Shaggy
Skyscraper–Demi Lovato
Dangerous Woman–Ariana Grande
Me, Myself and I–G-Eazy, Bebe Rexha
The Sound of Silence–Disturbed

Acknowledgements

First and foremost, thank you to God for granting me the gift of storytelling.

Thank you to my husband, Jim. Babe, I know you won't read this, but you don't know how much I love you. Your support has been truly amazing. It's so helpful when you do laundry or cook while I'm writing, and I'll never be able to thank you enough.

To my boys, Ethan and Evan (the real Evan). You light up my life and are truly a blessing.

To my editor, Tiffany. You are always such a joy to work with, and I always feel like I learn something with each book released. You're my editing goddess. :-)

To my publisher, Limitless! You guys have been so great to work with. From Lori to Jennifer to Jessica, no matter when I email you, even if it's a dumb question, I always get a response.

To Lydia, for always being such a great book pimp!

Again to my readers, because your support means so much to me. Thank you!

I know I'm forgetting people, which is typical. So thank you, thank you, thank you!

About the Author

A Midwesterner and self-proclaimed nerd, Evan has been an avid reader most of her life, but five years ago got bit by the writing bug, and it quickly became her addiction, passion and therapy. When the voices in her head give it a rest, she can always be found with her e-reader in her hand. Some of her favorites include, Shayla Black, Jaci Burton, Madeline Sheehan and Jamie Mcguire. Evan finds a lot of her inspiration in music, so if you see her wearing her headphones you know she means business and is in the zone.

During the day Evan works for a large homecare agency and at night she's superwoman. She's a wife to Jim and a mom to Ethan and Evan, a cook, a tutor, a friend and a writer. How does she do it? She'll never tell.

Facebook:
https://www.facebook.com/pages/Evan-Grace/626268640762539

Twitter:
https://twitter.com/Evan76Grace

Website:
http://www.authorevangrace.com/

Goodreads:
https://www.goodreads.com/author/show/7788444.Evan_Grace